"Maybe I Should Ask You What You Want."

His mouth curving in unconscious sensuality, he warned, "You might not like the answer."

"Try me."

"I . . . want . . . you."

Hayley instinctively pulled back, but his hand trapped hers. Locked as she was to him, she felt as if she were running at breakneck speed away from him, from all he represented.

"I don't know for how long," he added swiftly. "Maybe not long enough for you. Maybe not in a way you *need*. I can't make promises that would be impossible to keep—I wouldn't. But if it means anything to you, you're proof to me that I'm capable of falling in love again."

Dear Reader:

Romance readers have been enthusiastic about Silhouette Special Editions for years. And that's not by accident: Special Editions were the first of their kind and continue to feature realistic stories with heightened romantic tension.

The longer stories, sophisticated style, greater sensual detail and variety that made Special Editions popular are the same elements that will make you want to read book after book.

We hope that you enjoy this Special Edition today, and will enjoy many more.

The Editors at Silhouette Books

NATALIE BISHOP
Trial by Fire

Silhouette Special Edition

Published by Silhouette Books New York

America's Publisher of Contemporary Romance

For Mom and Dad

SILHOUETTE BOOKS
300 E. 42nd St., New York, N.Y. 10017

Copyright © 1985 by Natalie Bishop

Distributed by Pocket Books

ISBN: 0-373-09245-8

First Silhouette Books printing June, 1985

10 9 8 7 6 5 4 3 2 1

America's Publisher of Contemporary Romance

Printed in the U.S.A.

NATALIE BISHOP

lives within a stone's throw of her sister, Lisa Jackson, who is also a Silhouette author. Natalie and Lisa spend many afternoons together developing new plots and reading their best lines to each other.

Silhouette Books by Natalie Bishop

Saturday's Child (SE #178)
Lover or Deceiver (SE #198)
Stolen Thunder (SE #231)
Trial By Fire (SE #245)

Chapter One

". . . the facts of the case are obvious. You, members of the jury, have heard the evidence, and as reasonable, discerning citizens, I'm sure you will come to the same conclusions I have. Mr. Taft—"Hayley Sinclair walked from one side of the jury box to the other, allowing them another view of the defendant—"failed to live up to the responsibility of his position. As director and associate producer of the motion picture, *Pacifica,* Mr. Taft's moral and legal obligations were to ensure the safety of all personnel working on the picture. But it was as a direct result of his negligence that Carl Jeffries died."

Not a sound issued from any member of the jury, nor was there even the merest squeak of a chair from the defendant's table. Hayley didn't look in the direction of Kennedy Taft as she continued her summation, but she was acutely aware of his thoughtful expression and sharp green eyes. Those eyes had followed her every move throughout the trial.

"The tragedy could have been averted had Mr. Taft been more careful. But in his reckless need to meet Hollywood's, and the public's, demands for realism, Mr. Taft ignored his most important responsibility—the safety of human life. Nothing—nothing—could be more important."

Hayley paused, letting her words sink in. She could see Kennedy Taft in her peripheral vision: his silent grave face, his thick, vital, nearly black hair, his rigid jawline. As she turned she felt the full force of his gaze knifing between her shoulder blades.

"It would be easy to say it wasn't his fault," Hayley went on, very aware of the defense's arguments. "That the accident was out of his control, beyond the scope of his job. That Mr. Taft did everything humanly possible to minimize the risk of accidents.

"But Carl Jeffries is dead." Hayley looked into the face of each juror. "He drowned in the Clackamas River after leaping from a boat engulfed in flames. He was no match for that ruthless current. In actual fact, Carl Jeffries could barely swim. . . ." Hayley paused significantly, letting the jurors mentally visualize the tragedy. In a disbelieving voice, she asked, "Is that really *minimizing* risk?

"The director is the man ultimately responsible for safety during production of a film. The director of *Pacifica*, Mr. Kennedy Taft, is responsible. But Mr. Taft failed to uphold that responsibility. He failed to revere human life in his zeal to create an epic block-buster packed with dangerous special effects."

Hayley walked to the left side of the jury box, concentrating her attention on one particular juror whose sympathies seemed to lie with the defendant. It was crucial to win his allegiance.

She saw his skepticism and attacked the issue she felt was his biggest stumbling block. "My client is asking for a million dollars. Yes, that's a lot of money. More than most of us will ever see. But what about Lisa Jeffries, Carl Jeffries's nine-year-old daughter? Doesn't she deserve something? Is a million dollars even enough? What is the price for losing a father? One million? Two? Twenty . . . ?"

Hayley took a deep breath. "There is no price. We all know that. Members of the jury, when it comes down to dollars and cents, Mr. Taft's gross negligence really hits home. For no one can buy back Carl Jeffries's life. It's gone. All we can do now is try to compensate. Compensate and grieve. Thank you."

Hayley walked back to her table through a silent room, her steps echoing hollowly. She sat down next to the woman she was representing. Claudia Jeffries was the estranged wife of the deceased, a woman who hadn't wasted any time in filing suit against Titan Pictures as a whole—and Kennedy Taft, in particular —after she'd learned about her ex-husband's death. Hayley understood the woman's motivations only too well, but she believed, as did the other partners of Sinclair, Holmsby, and Layton, that Carl Jeffries's accident should have been prevented. A personal injury award to the deceased's wife would be a way to set a new precedent for safety during filmmaking.

The attorney for the defense, Robert T. Renton, a man imported by Taft from Los Angeles, rose to make his own closing statements. Hayley followed him with her eyes, mentally going over the trial from beginning to end. Had she been effective in winning the jury to her side? Had she exhausted every means of proving Kennedy Taft's culpability? Was there something else she could have done?

The suit against Titan Pictures was separate from the one against Taft. Hayley wasn't trying Titan's case herself, but the Taft decision would probably have an effect on its outcome.

Of their own volition, her eyes strayed to the defendant's chair. Kennedy Taft was a compelling, quiet man who had faced the alleged charges of the civil suit against him with a gravity and straightforwardness that Hayley had to admire. She felt a twinge of remorse that she was fighting on the opposite side, but she truly believed he had been negligent.

With a suddenness that left no time for Hayley to react, Kennedy Taft's eyes clashed with hers. For a long moment, while his attorney systematically battered down all of Hayley's carefully constructed arguments, his green gaze drove into her startled gray one. Hayley pulled her eyes away. *Let's get this over with,* she thought silently, conscious that Kennedy Taft was still staring at her.

The jury was in deliberation for two long weeks. During that time, Hayley's tension seemed to mount by the minute. She had trouble concentrating on anything besides the outcome.

The other partners and associates of her firm kept telling her what a wonderful job she'd done, how confident they felt that the jury would bring in a verdict in her client's favor. But Hayley was consumed with doubt. She always felt unsure when a jury took so much time deliberating, and now that feeling was magnified a thousandfold. This case was not the kind she usually tried. Portland, Oregon just didn't have famous Hollywood directors on trial. But the accident had happened here, during the filming, and Claudia Jeffries had filed the suit in Portland. Hayley had been lucky enough to be selected to try a case that would receive national attention. . . .

The jury was filing back in, their faces set and unreadable, and Hayley's heart began to beat faster. She refused to look at Kennedy Taft. In the back of the room, though there was no noise, Hayley imagined the clamor and excitement of the press. There were more newspeople collected for this trial than any trial she'd ever been at before.

"Have you reached a verdict?" the judge asked the jury.

"We have, Your Honor."

Claudia Jeffries leaned forward in tense expectation as the foreman of the jury read from a small slip of paper. Hayley's mouth was dry. She tried swallowing but couldn't. Unable to resist, she dared a glance at Kennedy Taft.

His hands were folded on top of the table, his

attention fixed on the thin scrap of paper in the foreman's hands. Hayley wondered fleetingly what his thoughts were.

"Your Honor, we have agreed to hold for the defendant, Kennedy Taft, and against the plaintiff, Claudia Jeffries."

There was a momentary hush, as if everyone in the room had been taken by surprise, then the judge's next words were drowned out in the babble of excitement from the spectators. Claudia Jeffries gasped and grabbed Hayley's forearm, her fingernails biting deeply.

"How could this happen?" she demanded, dazed. "How could you let this happen?"

Hayley was staring at Kennedy Taft. The iron control she'd seen in his straight spine had relaxed, and relief showed in the softening curve to his grim mouth. The press was besieging him, but he shook his head to all their questions.

"It's not over yet," Hayley tried to reassure her client. She was feeling slightly stunned herself. "You can appeal, and the chances are—"

"Appeal?" Claudia shook her head. "More waiting? I've waited long enough. Too long!"

She rose stiffly and Hayley stood up, too. Press people and spectators were swarming through the courtroom, and Hayley wanted to wait until all the hubbub died down before she and Claudia tried to leave.

"Claudia, let's sit down until the aisle clears," Hayley advised. "We're not defeated yet."

Claudia pursed her lips. Her face was white except

for two high spots of color on her cheeks. "I'm not defeated," she declared, moving away in spite of Hayley's protests. "But I'm not happy either, Miss Sinclair!"

Realizing her client was walking into a lion's den of reporters, Hayley tried to keep up with her. But Claudia Jeffries wasn't interested in waiting. She hustled her way through the crowd, heedless of Hayley's frantic efforts to keep up with her.

Hayley caught her at the main courthouse door. "Claudia," she warned in a low voice, "the press are going to swoop down on you as soon as they—"

"Mrs. Jeffries!"

Hayley touched Claudia's arm, trying to bypass the cluster of reporters heading their way. A young man, who'd detached himself from the crowd around Kennedy Taft first, was working his way toward them. "Keep walking," Hayley said tersely. "Don't look back, and don't wait for him. There's sure to be a lot more of them outside, but it's best if you don't say too much."

A wall of humanity impeded their progress through the courthouse doors, and suddenly they were surrounded by reporters. They were everywhere, barraging Claudia with questions.

"Are you surprised at the verdict, Mrs. Jeffries?"

"Are you going to appeal?"

Then, to Hayley, "How does it feel to lose to a renowned Los Angeles lawyer?"

Claudia opened her mouth to speak and Hayley mentally groaned. She was afraid of the damage a few careless words could create. "Of course, I'm going to appeal," Claudia said. "This is a slap in the face to both me and my daughter!"

"You don't think justice was served, then?"

Claudia touched a searching hand to the feathered layers of her brown hair and looked earnestly at the young woman who'd asked the last question. "I don't care about myself, but my daughter deserves far better than this. Her father's gone. She deserves to be compensated. Nothing can bring Carl back, of course, but something should be done to prevent this kind of thing from happening again. Don't you agree?"

The woman smiled. "What you're saying, then, is that you were more interested in winning to set a safety precedent, than for the monetary award."

"Why, yes. Of course."

Hayley tried to shepherd Claudia outside. She was aware that Claudia was trying to win the press and public sentiment to her side, but was afraid she might harm herself in the process. Some of the questions were double-edged and deadly.

Hayley's efforts were in vain. She was hindered and pushed and finally separated from her client. Forced to wait outside, under a gray and drizzling Portland sky, Hayley scanned the crowd by the doorway anxiously, hoping against hope that Claudia would break free.

She fumbled with the catch on her umbrella, then was forced down two more of the steps that angled around the courthouse by the growing mass of people outside. Her brain ticked off the seconds. She prayed Claudia would escape before she said something she'd regret.

A photographer at the bottom of the steps was taking pictures. Hayley was captured on film as soon as one of the reporters waved a microphone in front of her face. "Does your client plan to appeal, Miss Sinclair? How does she feel about the verdict?"

"You'll have to ask her yourself," Hayley answered with a restrained smile, inwardly vowing to get Claudia through this gauntlet of press people before that could happen. "She's disappointed, I'm sure."

"And what about you?"

"Naturally, I'm disappointed, too."

And she was. Very disappointed. Yet, her disappointment was edged with a certain amount of relief. As much as she believed film companies, producers, directors and everyone else involved in moviemaking were going to have to cut down on risk and make film production safer, Hayley wasn't entirely convinced that Kennedy Taft should have been the man to shoulder all the blame. She couldn't help imagining him—like Carl Jeffries—as a victim rather than a perpetrator.

"Will Sinclair, Holmsby, and Layton continue to represent Mrs. Jeffries?"

People were crowding around them, but instead of offering Hayley a chance to squeeze away from the dogged reporter, they stopped, interested in the little drama unfolding before them. Hayley began to feel impatient.

"If that's Mrs. Jeffries's wish," she said, seeing Claudia come through the door with a gaggle of eager press people. Hayley was sure her father, as senior partner of the law firm, would be eager to keep

Sinclair, Holmsby, and Layton's name in front of the public eye. What *she* had to do was rescue her client. "Excuse me. . . ."

"What about you? Will you be her prosecuting attorney?"

Hayley glanced quickly at her watch. "As an appeal hasn't been completely decided upon, any conjecture on my part would be pointless."

Before the reporter could ask another question, she turned away. She wished the drizzle would turn into a cloudburst, driving everyone from the scene.

"There's Mr. Taft!"

The cry went up and the reporter who'd nailed Hayley swept eagerly past her, pushing his way back up the steps to attack his new quarry.

Hayley paused for a moment. She studied Kennedy Taft carefully, memorizing his face for reasons she couldn't quite understand. She tilted the black arch of her umbrella backward to get a better look, noticing the tiny droplets of water that clung to his midnight-dark hair. Though she was sorry she'd lost the case, she couldn't honestly say she was unhappy that he'd won. . . .

The press were jostling him. Questions were being aimed like bullets. Claudia Jeffries may have been more than willing to speak out about the injustice she'd been served, but Kennedy Taft wasn't going to wallow in the glory of his victory. He merely raised a restraining palm and moved deliberately down the steps.

Then Taft saw Hayley. He hesitated, and to her dismay headed straight for her. All through the trial

Hayley had sensed his assessing eyes and had shuddered at the thought of what must be passing through his mind. She'd done everything in her power to show him as the guilty party; she'd wanted to win. Now, as his eyes sent silent messages to hers, Hayley expected to see simmering hostility, and she braced herself for the smug "I told you so" that was sure to come.

He stopped about four feet in front of her and smiled, a genuine smile of relief, weariness and admiration. Admiration for her?

He reached out and clasped her hand. "Well done, Miss Sinclair," he said, and Hayley stared at him in disbelief for a full five seconds.

The television cameras captured everything.

Chapter Two

*H*ayley pulled the pins from her hair and let it fall out in a dark blond, sodden curtain. She ran her fingers through it, further destroying the sleek, sophisticated illusion she'd worked so hard to prepare that morning. It was a sad fact, but Hayley had learned early in her law career that it helped establish credibility in a jury's eyes if she deemphasized her femininity. A severe chignon and tailored suit were her courtroom attire.

But it hardly mattered now. For her, the trial was over. And, according to Claudia Jeffries, it was over for Sinclair, Holmsby, and Layton as well.

Summoned to her father's inner office, Hayley had overheard the anger in Claudia's strident voice even before she knocked.

". . . I wasn't properly represented," she'd accused, her voice carrying easily into the outer hall. "And you're to blame! Why I consented to using that young, inexperienced girl, I'll never know. It was a mistake. A mistake I have no intention of paying for!"

"Hayley has more than enough experience," Jason Sinclair's soothing voice had reminded Claudia. He didn't bother to point out that it had been Claudia herself who'd demanded that a woman represent her. "She's thirty-two and very qualified. You seemed to be impressed with her qualifications," he added.

"I was. Until she lost the case for me."

"The jury decided, Mrs. Jeffries." Hayley's father was stern.

Claudia laughed humorlessly. "Your daughter's ineffectual representation decided them, Mr. Sinclair."

Unable to bear eavesdropping any longer, Hayley had rapped loudly. Her stomach was twisting in knots, and at her father's "Come in," she inhaled deeply and entered the plush, Danish-modern interior of his office.

"Ah, Hayley . . ." Jason Sinclair motioned her to a chair next to Claudia. "I've been explaining Mrs. Jeffries's appeal rights to her."

Claudia abruptly stood up, barely giving Hayley a glance. "I know my rights already. And I know when I've been taken advantage of." Her tone was withering and full of contempt. "You people used me to get media attention. Your law firm's been hyped by the press for months! Better than money, isn't it? Free publicity? You didn't even prepare for this case."

"That's not true." Hayley could stand no more. "I prepared night and day for this trial. Everyone here pitched in. If you really believe we were after publicity, then you have to know that we wouldn't want to lose. A defeat for you is a defeat for Sinclair, Holmsby, and Layton as well."

"Well, then my error was in ever having you represent me at all," she declared. "I must have been crazy to expect an unknown Portland girl to win against a noted Los Angeles attorney." She pulled her gloves on fiercely, barely waiting for Jason Sinclair to retrieve her raincoat and help her on with it. At the door she paused theatrically. "When I appeal, I'll be using another firm. Good day."

It had been brutal icing to an already disastrous day. Hayley's father had tried to convince her that she wasn't to blame, but his arguments weren't particularly strong. She'd gotten the impression that he was disappointed in her, too.

And reminding Claudia Jeffries that she'd specifically selected Hayley because she'd wanted someone local, someone who was established and well liked within Oregon's law circles . . . well, that had been out of the question, too. Claudia Jeffries's mind was made up.

Hayley looked at the clock now and sighed. She'd promised Matt Andrews that she'd go out for a "victory" celebration with him that evening. Matt was an associate at Sinclair, Holmsby, and Layton, and a personal friend of Hayley's. He'd been so positive that she'd win—and so insistent that she make arrangements to celebrate with him—that Hayley had reluctantly given in. Now, as she turned on the taps to the shower, she wished she'd hung firm. The last thing she felt like doing was toasting her defeat.

Could she have done something differently? Hayley asked herself, as the hot spray needled against her skin. Presented her case some other way? Said something else to swing the jury to her side?

Hayley went over it all again in her mind. No, to the best of her knowledge she'd done everything she could to win the case. She'd blocked and torn apart the defense's key points and arguments, then pushed to make her own carry more weight.

The memory of Kennedy Taft made her feel vaguely uneasy. It was true that she believed he was something of a victim himself. Was it possible that that belief had affected the way she'd tried the case?

No.

Hayley shook her head under the running water. Victim or no, Kennedy Taft was responsible. She'd wanted to win the case against him. There'd been a lot of pressure put on her *to* win. And she'd done her level best to do just that. Claudia Jeffries's unfair implications had just gotten under her skin.

Rubbing her wet hair dry with a towel, Hayley tried to work up some enthusiasm for the evening ahead. The one thing she was not going to do was mope about the way things had turned out—especially in front of Matt and the other associates.

While she was dressing Hayley thought about turning on the evening news. She was reluctant, because she knew what she would see: herself. She could remember only too clearly the television cameras pointed in her direction.

Out of some perverse sense of dedication, she finally switched it on. *Better to know the worst,* she told herself with a grimace.

She saw herself, looking hopelessly feminine and helpless, fumbling with the catch on her umbrella. She saw the look of impatience that crossed her face when the reporter cornered her, and read her own lips though the newscast had been dubbed over. Then she saw herself turn to watch Kennedy Taft come down the steps.

It was the cameraman's good fortune, and Hayley's plain bad luck, that he had caught that long, long moment when Kennedy Taft's eyes sparred with hers. Hayley found herself holding her breath as she watched his image walk toward hers, his hand reach out and clasp hers. The look on her face at that crucial instant said it all. She'd been struck dumb with amazement, and had barely managed a choked "Thank you," to his compliment. Taft's smile had dared to grow wider.

". . . it looks like Kennedy Taft knows how to be a gracious winner," the anchorman was saying. "It seems evident at this point that Mrs. Jeffries will appeal the decision. Whether Miss Hayley Sinclair, of Sinclair, Holmsby, and Layton, will be her prosecuting attorney again is still unknown. . . ."

Hayley groaned in utter embarrassment. Seeing the replay on television only made it that much worse. Had she really looked as inept and flustered as she imagined? Remembering how she'd fretted that Claudia Jeffries would do something she would regret, Hayley dipped her forehead into her palm. Dear God, *she'd* been the one who'd ended up looking like a fool!

The view outside the front window of Kennedy's hotel suite was spectacular, even with the cloud cover. A wide portion of the Willamette River could be seen between two of the modest skyscrapers that made up Portland's unique skyline. The inner section of the Steel Bridge was slowly lowering; the huge freighter had already passed beneath its span.

"I cannot believe your good luck, pal," Gordon Woodrow said for the third time. Kennedy heard the rustle of ice in the ice bucket, then the clink of several cubes against a glass. "Sure you won't have one?" Gordon asked. "Man, you deserve it. You must carry some kind of talisman. I cannot believe your good luck!"

Kennedy turned his head and regarded Gordon thoughtfully. He was Titan Pictures' assistant production head, the man the film company had sent to keep abreast of the Taft trial. Titan was very eager to wash their hands of the whole situation. They'd tried to settle out of court with Claudia Jeffries, but the woman had flatly refused. Kennedy wondered who at Sinclair, Holmsby, and Layton had offered Mrs. Jeffries that advice.

"You make it sound like you believe I was guilty," Kennedy said dryly.

"What has guilt got to do with anything?" Gordon responded philosophically. "This isn't a criminal trial.

No one's broken the law. It's just that for a while I was afraid the jury would forget the real issue, and decide against you just to compensate Jeffries's kid. I mean, this way she doesn't get a dime."

Kennedy fell silent. He didn't like the way things had turned out for Lisa Jeffries. As far as her mother went . . . well, his heart wasn't breaking for Claudia. Hell, he'd tried to settle with the woman, too! The last thing he'd wanted to do was go to trial, for God's sake. Who—*Who*—had talked Claudia Jeffries out of that settlement?

"You know," Gordon said, settling himself into one of the leather-cushioned chairs around a large rectangular table, "I'm still surprised things went this far."

"You just echoed my thoughts." Kennedy turned away from the window, feeling restless.

"I mean, who would gamble like that? You know what they say about a bird in the hand. . . ."

Kennedy shrugged. "I don't know. I don't like it though."

Gordon looked up, surprised. "You don't like it? Are you crazy? You don't owe that woman a cent! She was just trying to take advantage of the situation. You know that. She and her husband barely spoke to one another."

Kennedy wouldn't have explained to Gordon how responsible he felt even if he could have expressed it in words. True, Carl Jeffries hadn't been authorized to be on that boat when it burst into flames. Had anyone really believed he would have been, given the man's poor swimming skills and the ferocious Clackamas River current? But the whole situation forced Kennedy to wonder if the tragedy wasn't partly his fault after all. . . .

He'd immediately fired the man who'd told Jeffries to set the boat aflame as soon as he'd sorted out what had happened; but, by then of course, it was too late for Carl. Kennedy had never dreamed that Bill Baines, the man he'd put in charge of the explosion, would be so foolhardy and negligent as to allow an inexperienced swimmer like Carl Jeffries anywhere near the boat-scene filming site.

The nightmare had gotten worse when Claudia Jeffries decided to sue. If a finger of guilt should be pointed somewhere, it should have been at Bill Baines, Kennedy felt. The trouble was, Baines had very little money, and probably minimal liability insurance, and therefore was not a good prospect for a civil suit. Kennedy Taft and Titan Pictures, on the other hand, were prime candidates. . . .

Kennedy's mouth tightened into a grim line. Things were so very seldom fair. "Lisa Jeffries is only nine years old," he said tightly. "The prosecution was right on one thing—she deserves something."

"It's not your problem, buddy. Okay? Let's just get through this thing." Gordon glanced at his watch, tossed off the rest of his drink and stood up. "I've got to leave. My flight's in an hour. Sure you won't change your mind and pack it in here? I think you need out of this town."

"No. I'll go back Monday as I planned." He didn't add that there were a few loose ends he wanted to tie up. Gordon wouldn't have understood.

Kennedy's attorney was leaving that evening as well

and, rationally, he knew there was no earthly reason for him to stay either. But he couldn't go . . . not yet.

Unconsciously reading Kennedy's thoughts, Gordon said, "Well, if you're gonna stay—have some fun, at least. You know that place I told you about? The Den? That's where all the speculation will be going on. You might even see the lovely—and newly defeated—prosecuting attorney there."

Kennedy regarded Gordon tolerantly. "Now why would I want to run into her?"

"I can think of half a dozen reasons. And from what showed on the tube—so can you."

Kennedy scowled at him, but Gordon was unperturbed. "Just don't rock the boat at this juncture, okay?" he advised.

Kennedy made a disgusted sound and strode to the bar. "You don't even deserve an answer."

"Okay, okay." Gordon lifted his palms in mock defense. "See you back on the planet. . . ."

Kennedy poured himself a neat Scotch after Gordon left, brooding silently for several minutes. Back on the planet. Gordon felt anyplace outside of California's borders was outer space. He sometimes felt that way himself, only in the reverse. To Kennedy, the film industry was an alien world, one which didn't quite jibe with the mold of society. But it was a world he fit into quite naturally, and a world he rarely exited—unless he was forced to.

Still, he was fully aware of what went on outside the plastic fantasy of moviemaking—it just wasn't the place where he earned his living, developed his creations. The trial had caused a collision between Kennedy's two worlds. He'd had to drop his current projects, and delegate authority to others. At first he'd been anxious and frustrated, but now . . . for some strange, inexplicable reason, he wasn't quite ready to go back yet.

Why not?

Kennedy had no answer. The closest thing he could come up with was that, as Gordon had alluded, he was interested in seeing Hayley Sinclair again. And the insanity of that made him reject that theory as quickly as he'd thought of it.

Kennedy swirled his drink. Unfortunately, honesty prevented him from banishing it outright. He'd been very aware of Miss Hayley Sinclair throughout the trial, so aware that he'd been unable to feel as outraged at Claudia Jeffries as he perhaps should have. And that awareness had made him want to congratulate her, to let her know that he admired her, respected her, even though she'd been on the opposing side. The television tape had been more damning than he'd wanted, but at least the deed was done.

And you'd be out of your mind to try and take this any further, he reminded himself harshly.

Kennedy sank into the luxurious, red leather couch, resting his head on its back, his gaze centered unseeingly on the ceiling. He thought back to the first time he'd set eyes on Hayley Sinclair.

It had been at the deposition. She'd been eager to establish a friendly relationship with him, and though he knew it was her way of ferreting out his weaknesses, Kennedy had been impressed by the solemn gray-eyed woman with the sun-streaked blond hair. There was a certain freshness and honesty that radiated from her that both intrigued and concerned him. He remembered worrying, rather unrealistically, that the jury would side with her on appearances alone.

The deposition was the only time he'd spoken to her directly—until he'd gotten on the witness stand. It was still possible for him to recall every inflection he'd heard in her clear, precise voice at that first encounter.

"You were actually at the film site when the accident occurred?" she'd asked him, her gaze occasionally slanting to the thick file opened in front of her.

"I'm the director," he'd answered with a touch of anger, offended by the subtle rebuke the question had implied. Of course he'd been there.

"That doesn't answer my question, Mr. Taft."

Kennedy had had to keep reminding himself of two things. One: Hayley Sinclair was a Portland attorney, who not only didn't know him, but didn't know his near fanatacism about being at the film site. Two: Just because she was beautiful, and obviously intelligent, didn't necessarily mean she wasn't treacherous—not only because she was the prosecuting attorney, but because she was a woman as well. . . .

"I was at the film site," he finally answered tightly.

"Did you actually see the accident?"

"I saw the explosion, and what I thought was someone jumping into the water." He picked his words carefully, aware of the pitfalls of offering more than short, succinct responses.

"What you *thought* was someone jumping into the water?" Hayley's question was quick.

"At that point, Miss Sinclair, I wasn't sure what I saw. But an actor—or a stunt double—jumping into the river was not part of the script."

Kennedy's attorney sniffed disapprovingly, and Hayley Sinclair's clear gray eyes regarded him silently for a few moments before she asked, "What was the first thing you did after you witnessed the 'jump'?"

"I started running to the river's edge, yelling like mad for help. It took a few minutes—not long— before a small boat was dispatched with expert divers aboard."

Hayley nodded. "And what were you doing while this was happening?"

He looked her straight in the eye, determined to tell the truth, stating the facts as he remembered them without embellishing, or trying subtly to plead his innocence. "I was stripping off my clothes, Miss Sinclair. If someone was in that river, I was going to go after him."

Kennedy's attorney, Robert T. Renton, warned him with a rigid glare that Kennedy had no trouble seeing out of his peripheral vision. He also saw the slight shake of his head, and heard him inhale between his teeth. But Kennedy's eyes stayed glued to Hayley Sinclair's face.

"But you didn't go in the water," she reminded him.

"No."

"Why not?"

Kennedy took a deep breath, remembering. "Because they pulled Carl's body out before I could," he said softly.

There was a pain-filled silence, broken only by Renton's pointed cough. Kennedy knew the last thing his attorney wanted was for things to get emotional, yet it was an emotional issue.

Hayley tried to pass over the charged moment by flipping through her file. When she looked up again, Kennedy's eyes were waiting for her. Then she dropped the bomb. "Were you aware that Carl Jeffries could barely swim?"

"No."

"Had you asked him?"

Kennedy felt everyone in the room tighten up, as if they were mentally leaning forward, tense and eager for his answer. He wondered if, by virtue of her womanhood, Hayley would be willing to listen to his explanation. His jaw tensed, then he said firmly, "No."

The hardness that entered her eyes made him realize he could never let himself underestimate her. If he did, he'd be lost. "Wouldn't you think that would be a reasonable question to ask someone working near a river, Mr. Taft? Especially one as dangerous as the Clackamas?"

His gaze didn't waver. "Yes."

"Then, why didn't you ask it?"

There was no way to disguise the truth. "Because I did not know Mr. Jeffries was working at the site," Kennedy said tensely.

Hayley's fine brow creased in puzzlement. "But you were the director."

Kennedy could see the direction her questioning was taking, but was powerless to forestall it. "Yes."

"Then why didn't you know?"

He was uncertain whether she was really curious, or whether this line of questioning was merely a rehearsal for the trial. "Because he wasn't the man responsible for the explosives. Bill Baines was the man appointed to the job."

And when I realized his gross negligence and irresponsibility, I fired him on the spot, Kennedy thought.

But he didn't say it aloud. Hayley Sinclair probably knew it already anyway. And she was the one asking the questions.

"Did Bill Baines report directly to you?"

"Yes."

At that point Renton rose abruptly, adjusting the crease in his slacks. He glanced pointedly at his watch. "Ah, could we stop at this point? Or is there anything else you need, Miss Sinclair?"

It was obvious to everyone concerned that Renton was worried about the direction of the interview. Hayley gave him a frosty smile, asserted that she did indeed have a few more questions, then proceeded to ask them, one by one. Kennedy had to admire her fortitude; she wasn't about to give in to pressure.

Eventually she placed her file back in her briefcase with a final-sounding snap. "I think this will take care of everything, for now," she said, shaking Renton's hand before turning to Kennedy.

For an instant, one brief millisecond, he thought he saw uncertainty in her eyes. Then it was gone, and she clasped his hand firmly with her delicate one. "Thank you," she said, the soft rustle of nylon and silk following her from the room.

Renton had dolefully shaken his head. "You're going to cook your own goose if you don't let up, Kennedy."

"The truth is the truth, no matter how you dress it up."

"And we're going to trial," Renton said shortly. "Keep that in mind."

Kennedy had. But at the trial, even though there was a lot at stake—money, his reputation, the reaction of the film companies after they heard the verdict—Kennedy still didn't regret that first exchange with Hayley. He'd told the truth, nothing more, nothing less. And during the midst and heat of everything, as incredible as it was, he found himself wondering about *her*. What her life was like. Who her friends were. Had she ever been married? Did she have any children? Was there a man in her life? A lover?

Kennedy tossed down the rest of his drink, then shook his head, swearing softly at his unbelievable susceptibility. What was wrong with him? Just because Hayley Sinclair was an attractive prosecuting attorney wasn't any reason for him to fantasize about her. But, he thought, a smile curving self-deprecatingly across his lips, that was exactly what he'd been doing.

As much as he wanted to deny it, he'd been attracted to her from the start. And that attraction had colored how he'd felt about the whole trial.

Luckily, he hadn't been the lawyer; he wasn't certain he could have fought that lovely lady head to head.

And, if he was completely honest with himself, when the deposition was over, he'd been left with an uneasy feeling that hadn't all been because he felt Hayley Sinclair's honesty and appearance could win her the jurors' hearts and minds. The plain truth was that he'd been very eager to see her again. . . .

Kennedy sighed, and frowned into his glass. Well, what was stopping him now? *That's why you stayed in Portland, isn't it?* he taunted himself. Before the trial, seeing Hayley Sinclair had been out of the question. But now? Now that it was all over?

He couldn't think of a reason in the world why he shouldn't see her.

The Den of Antiquity was an intimate bar and eatery, patronized by the up-and-coming in downtown Portland's business world. It was a favorite meeting place for Sinclair, Holmsby, and Layton's partners and associates, and Hayley wasn't really surprised when Matt parked his car in the underground lot. What she didn't tell him was that the Den was about the last place in the world she wanted to go tonight. The well-meant empathy from her friends was something she would have liked to put off for another day.

As Matt touched her elbow, guiding Hayley through the ornate oak-plank doors decorated with iron grillwork, he finally noticed her pensive quietness. "Feel lousy, don't you?" he asked.

"Worse than lousy," Hayley responded with a sigh. "I feel like a failure."

"A failure!" Matt clucked his tongue. "Give yourself a break, Hayley. You were fabulous." The "I know you're just trying to make me feel better" look that Hayley shot him prompted Matt to add, "You've lost cases before. This is just one more."

Hayley preceded him inside, following the maître d' to a corner table that offered some privacy. "Easy for you to say, Matt. *This* was the big one."

"You done good, kid. I mean it. You were—and still are—the best."

Hayley managed a smile. For the first time that day she felt the pressure of the trial recede. Maybe it was the comfortable surroundings of the Den—the bookcases filled with gilt-edged volumes, the authentic antiques, the suit of armor standing in attendance by the front door. Hayley had spent many other post-trial evenings here, often accepting the congratulations of her friends and associates for a job well done.

"Claudia Jeffries wouldn't agree with you," Hayley answered him, remembering the scene in her father's office.

"Mmmm . . . yeah . . . I heard." Matt settled himself across from her, leaning forward on his elbows. "Don't let it get to you, Hayley. Claudia Jeffries doesn't know what's good for her. The woman has got a lot to learn. A *lot* to learn."

"I don't know. She seems to know exactly what she wants. Maybe I just didn't read her correctly."

"Would you stop that?" Matt motioned for a waiter, then turned back to Hayley. "If you made a mistake, it was only that you forgot one important point: Claudia Jeffries didn't ever give a damn about whether it was safe or not at the film site. That woman sees one thing, and one thing only: money. Anything else she says is bull. She picked you because she thought you were her best ticket to success. If she's angry now, well, it's her problem. She has no reason to be. You did a damned good job."

Hayley smiled. "Even if I can't believe a word of what you say, thanks."

"Believe *every* word," Matt encouraged. "What would you like to drink?"

Hayley looked up. The waiter was standing by expectantly. She ordered a glass of white wine, and reminded herself never to forget what a good friend Matt was. Matt was currently going through a very emotional divorce; he was still in love with his wife. The pressure from the divorce tended to make him moody, and Hayley had to walk on eggshells around him more often than not just to keep the peace. Lately, their working relationship had been strained for the same reason, and Hayley had accepted Matt's invitation as a way to pour oil on troubled waters as much as anything else.

"I wonder if the Taft entourage is still in town," Matt mused, polishing off his second Scotch and soda while Hayley was still sipping her first glass of wine. He ordered another, and Hayley inwardly hoped Matt wasn't going to keep drinking and go all moody on her again.

"I don't see any reason why they'd stay," Hayley observed. She, for one, would be glad when they all returned to California.

"I saw the man from Titan Pictures here the other night, did I tell you?"

Hayley blinked. "Here?"

Matt nodded. "Right smack dab in the middle of the trial. I actually thought he might say something to one of us, but he just ordered a couple of drinks and left. Maybe Portland's a little tame for his tastes," he added waspishly.

Hayley visualized Gordon Woodrow and wondered if Matt might not be right about the stocky studio producer. She'd gotten the impression that the whole thing had been one great big yawn for him, and that his only worry was the size of Titan's bill. The reason for the claims against Titan Pictures never seemed to enter his head.

Hayley had been much more impressed by Robert T. Renton, Taft's attorney. He was factual, no-nonsense, precise and a far cry from the flamboyant Hollywood lawyer she'd expected. Even so, she had to admit, Kennedy Taft himself had made the greatest impression upon her.

"It's a shame they got off scot-free," Matt said, dragging Hayley back to the present. "A man's dead and they just say, 'Ho, hum. Too bad.' I think it's a crime."

Matt ordered another drink and Hayley grew more uncomfortable. Her friend had been drinking a lot lately. She watched him down half of it, and finally asked, "Matt, is anything wrong?"

"Wrong? What d'ya mean, wrong?"

Hayley lifted her shoulders. "I think you know."

His expression darkened and his lips compressed. For a moment, Hayley wondered if she hadn't pushed him too far. Though they were friends, there were personal areas of each other's lives they never trespassed into.

After a moment, Matt shrugged. "No big deal, if I think I deserve a few drinks," he said lightly.

"No big deal," she agreed. "But it could be."

"I don't need another conscience."

His aggressive tone made Hayley lapse into silence. She wasn't afraid, but she was worried. Was Matt's deteriorating relationship with Sheryl the reason he was seeking refuge in alcohol? She thought he'd gotten beyond that stage. Was it something else?

Hayley was glad when several people she knew stopped by the table to offer their comments and opinions about the trial—a situation she'd desperately wanted to avoid only a few hours before. But Matt's mood switch and now surly company made her uneasy, and a headache was beginning to pulse at her temples.

What a day! she thought with an inward sigh. She longed to be home, alone, and was about to suggest the same to Matt when she heard the Den's door open and close. She looked up just in time to see Kennedy Taft walk into the restaurant, his long stride carrying him to the book-lined shelves of the antique, oak-paneled bar.

"What's the matter?" Matt asked, at her sharp intake of breath.

"Nothing."

A feeling of dread was uncoiling within her. Hayley leaned back into the curved contours of the leather booth, and prayed that Taft would go by without seeing her. Why she harbored such paranoia, she refused to analyze. But after the events of the day, she felt she deserved to avoid what could only be another uncomfortable scene.

But Matt had seen her expression. He craned his neck to see what she'd seen, focusing in on Kennedy Taft.

"Ohhhh . . . ," he said knowingly. "So that's it."

Normally Matt would sympathize with her need for privacy, but after his heavy consumption of alcohol Hayley wasn't certain how he would react. "I just don't feel like running into him right now. Do you blame me? And what if someone from the press is here? No need to make the eleven o'clock news, too."

"Relax. He's probably looking for someone a little more willing than you."

Hayley's brow puckered. She wasn't quite sure what Matthew meant by that. She'd opened her mouth to ask him, when he suddenly leaned forward. "Get ready, girl," he whispered, with more enjoyment than Hayley felt the situation warranted. "He's heading this way."

The soft moan that escaped her was an expression of how tired she felt. She wished she had the nerve to face Kennedy Taft, and say, "Not now. I've battled you for weeks. But I'm not ready now. . . ."

"Mr. Taft," Matt called out as he moved into their

view again. Hayley's lips parted in dismay at Matt's intervention. What was he trying to do to her?

"Matthew," she whispered through clenched teeth.

But Taft had heard the hail. He walked to their booth, and through a supreme effort of will, Hayley managed a stiff smile of greeting.

His return smile was little short of an impertinent grin. Hayley's feeling of dread increased.

"Hello, Miss Sinclair," he said.

To Hayley, his ease and naturalness was almost comedic, as if this was the kind of thing that happened to him every day.

"Mr. Taft," she acknowledged, trying to match his tone. She turned slightly, to include Matt. "This is Matthew Andrews, an associate at my firm. Matt, I'm sure you recognize Mr. Kennedy Taft."

"The defendant," Kennedy said dryly.

Kennedy's irreverence appealed to Matt. Hayley's hopes sank as she saw her only ally shake hands fervently with Kennedy.

"Ah, yes," Matt responded, grinning. "The defendant." He cast a sly glance toward Hayley that boded trouble. "I've heard a lot about you. Why don't you join us?"

Kennedy's gaze slid to Hayley. She felt him assessing her once more, and she raised her eyes to meet his blatant stare. She was furious with Matt. How *could* he? After she'd told him how she felt? Matt's earlier goodwill seemed to have abandoned him. Now Hayley was on her own.

"Yes, do," Hayley said, her jaw tight. But her voice

sounded poised enough. Matthew had given her no choice but to echo his request, and innate politeness helped her to follow through. But if Kennedy could guess what was going through her mind . . .

A slow grin spread across Kennedy's rugged face. "If I make you that uncomfortable maybe I should leave."

Hayley flushed. His perception—not to mention his audacity!—made her feel like a fraud. She wondered if he was enjoying himself at her expense. Since Matthew wasn't budging—quite the contrary, he was looking intensely interested and eager—Hayley was forced to scoot across her seat. "Sit down," she invited, extremely conscious of those silver-green eyes that dared hers. "I'm surprised you're still in town, Mr. Taft," she said. "I thought you'd be winging your way back to Hollywood by now."

Matthew's brows lifted in surprise at Hayley's tone. Her head throbbed. She was feeling hemmed in on all sides.

"I thought I might stay over a few more days," Kennedy replied easily, unperturbed. "Portland's a beautiful city."

"Is that why you picked it for *Pacifica?*"

His searching look made Hayley reach for her wineglass as a distraction. She knew he was wondering if there was a hidden rebuke in those words, and if she was totally honest with herself, she would admit there was.

"Why did you stay on?" Matthew asked.

Kennedy shrugged. He was so close to Hayley that

his suit coat brushed the gathered folds of her silk sleeve. Hayley shrank within herself without moving.

"After the trial, I just wasn't that eager to race back. I thought I might give myself some R and R. There's nothing pressing for me to get back to right now."

"No more movies?" Hayley managed to hold his level gaze. She could see the rough texture of his skin, the deep tan that came from spending a lot of time outdoors. Tiny lines of disillusionment bracketed his mouth, as if all of his experiences hadn't been pleasant ones.

"I'm on hiatus," he said with a smile. "Nothing on the boards for a few more weeks. I wasn't sure how long the trial would last."

Hayley picked up her long-stemmed glass. "Well, it's over," she said, not wishing to rehash the events. "I guess congratulations are due."

The waiter rescued Hayley at that moment, taking Kennedy's order. Hayley felt a thin film of sweat break out on her shoulders and between her breasts. This was even worse than the trial.

Hayley sensed that she'd disappointed Kennedy in some way. She told herself she didn't care. She refused to let her guard down for an instant, although, rationally, she was aware that the foe she was fighting was only imagined.

But she was leery of Kennedy's reasons for hanging around Portland. She couldn't believe he was playing this "just one of the guys" routine for no reason. Just what his advantage was at this point, she couldn't guess. Unless, of course, he still didn't know that Claudia Jeffries had dropped Hayley as her attorney.

Matthew coughed significantly. "Well, this has been great, but I've got to make a phone call. If you'll excuse me . . ."

Hayley's eyes jerked despairingly to Matthew's, but he had already slid from the booth, heading in another direction. She watched him leave with a mixture of fury and disbelief. He was purposely throwing her to the wolves, of that she was certain. Her hands balled into impotent fists beneath the table, and she made a mental note to kill Matthew when he returned.

Watching him disappear around the corner, Kennedy moved from his place next to Hayley and sat down opposite her.

"I've spoiled your evening," he said, searching Hayley's face. "I'm sorry. That wasn't my intention."

Hayley thought how strange her relationship with this man was. "What *was* your intention?" she asked, before she could lose her courage.

His smile was self-deprecating. "Not to spoil your evening."

She realized he thought he'd interrupted a romantic date, and, for some reason, she couldn't let him go on thinking that way. "Don't worry about it. Our evening wasn't going that well anyway." Seeing his look, she added candidly, "Things have been pretty bleak around Sinclair, Holmsby, and Layton today."

"Touché. I imagine I'm about the last person in the world you want to speak to tonight."

"You, and everybody else," Hayley agreed, softening her words with a smile. "No offense. It's just been that kind of day."

"None taken. If it means anything to you—which it probably won't—"he bowed his head in charming humility—"you impressed me more than anyone has in a long time. I'd heard you were a skillful lawyer, but I admit I was surprised at how skillful."

His praise was so unexpected that Hayley didn't know quite how to react. "Easy for you to say now," she murmured lightly.

"Easy for me to say anyway."

"Why are you here, Mr. Taft?"

Hayley had never been one to beat around the bush. More than once she'd startled people with her abrupt methods of cutting to the heart of an issue.

But Kennedy was relieved by her forthrightness. Instead of being put off, he grinned with real enjoyment. He'd had a feeling about this woman from the beginning. There was no coyness in her, no hidden undercurrents that could drag a man down. His appreciation of her, something he'd thought would dwindle with time, only grew greater every time they met.

God, he thought, trying to minimize his attraction to her, *why does it have to be this woman?*

"Because I needed a change of pace," he answered, admiring Hayley's unconscious elegance. In his world, women wore the strangest things: loose-shouldered, tight-hipped designer gowns in gold lamé; casually draped furs with mid-calf jeans and striped socks; gaudy jewelry; picture-painted nails; art deco silkscreened T-shirts in colors that assaulted the eye. . . . Kennedy had never thought of himself as particularly conservative, but after growing accustomed to some of the trendy attire sported in Southern California, he found Hayley's tailored suits, soft silk blouses and subdued but rich colors a welcome relief.

Warning himself not to make too much of the things about her that appealed to him, Kennedy found himself intrigued nevertheless.

"Actually," he admitted, noticing the solemnness of her gray eyes, "I was hoping to see you again."

Hayley fought her instinctive reaction: the gasp that caught in her throat, the shock that registered on her face. She was amazed at his incredible bluntness. "Why? The trial's over."

"That's exactly why. The trial is over." There was no amusement on his face now. "You're no longer Claudia Jeffries's attorney."

So he'd heard. Hayley wasn't really surprised. Claudia had probably informed the press at the first possible opportunity. Still, she felt a tiny pain, a twisting knife of guilt and uneasiness that had a lot to do with her present companion.

"So it's safe to talk to me now?" Hayley's words tasted bitter.

"Why are you so angry about this trial?"

His words cut to her heart. "Because I like to think justice has been served, Mr. Taft," she fired back. "And I'm not certain it has been this time."

"What justice? We're talking about a civil suit,

aren't we?" Hayley's unfairness struck a well-aimed arrow to Kennedy's Achilles' heel, his own dissatisfaction with the way things had turned out. "What gives you the right to pass judgment?" he demanded.

"Lisa Jeffries," Hayley answered coldly.

"That's hardly your jurisdiction, counselor. Since when are you judge and jury, too?"

Tension sparked in the air between them. Hayley wondered how things had gotten so blown out of proportion. She was appalled at her lack of professionalism.

Not waiting for Matt, she grabbed her coat. "Excuse me," she murmured.

"Wait."

Kennedy's hand caught her wrist. Hayley would have forcefully yanked herself away if she'd been anywhere else. But she could see heads turning and, with iron control, she stood still while he rose beside her. "Let go of me, Mr. Taft," she said with a cold smile that had served its purpose on more than one occasion. "I don't want a scene any more than you do. There are people I know here. And they certainly know who you are."

Some of her frigid anger lost its effect when Hayley realized he was barely touching her. His hand dropped instantly.

He shook his head in disbelief. "Miss Sinclair, the last thing I want to do is fight with you. I've done enough of that in the past few weeks to last me a lifetime and more." That crooked, self-mocking grin slid across his face again. "It's hard for me to believe anyone is truly as dedicated to conviction as you seem to be. Somehow I thought lawyers were always in it for the money."

"I'm not totally selfless, Mr. Taft."

Kennedy laughed. "Honesty's your best quality." She saw his eyes travel slowly down the outline of her body. "Well," he drawled, humor glinting in the silver-green depths of his eyes, "maybe not your best . . ."

Hayley was at a loss. Her inclination to leave kept her on her feet, but his unaffected charm rooted her to the spot. "Do you know," she said with a sigh, "that I have no idea in the world how to talk with you?"

"Yes." His directness was disarming.

Hayley made an exasperated sound and turned her head from side to side, searching the room, willing to see anything but Kennedy Taft.

"Let's leave," he suggested, tossing money for the bill onto the table.

"Are you crazy?" Hayley snatched up her own purse, determined not to let him pay.

"I'll buy you a drink at the Cheswick. But let's get out of here now. Too many people you know," he pointed out wickedly.

"I'm with Matt."

Kennedy's brows raised in silent inquiry. Hayley knew it was more than obvious that she wasn't. She'd said as much. And Matt's desertion was impossible to ignore.

"Leaving with you would be suicidal to my reputation," Hayley said, wishing the idea sounded less appealing than it did. She didn't understand herself at all. "Surely you can see that."

"Mm-hm. And I also see that you're dying to get out of here, Hayley." His unexpected use of her first name stopped her from trying to retake her seat. "I only have a few days left here. I'd really appreciate a chance to talk to you before I go."

Matt chose that inopportune moment to reappear. He sized up the situation instantly. "You're leaving?"

"No, Matt. Mr. Taft's leaving."

The frown that instantly creased Matt's brow bothered Hayley. Why was he foisting her off on Kennedy Taft? Couldn't he see the consequences of such an action?

"I called Sheryl," he said, offering some insight into his motives. "She wants to see me right away, so I asked her to meet me here. Do you mind?"

Hayley stared at Matt. To Hayley's knowledge, Sheryl hadn't met him face-to-face for several months. Why *now?*

"The fates are against me," Hayley murmured under her breath.

"What?"

"Never mind." She tied the sash around her coat. "I think this would be a good time for me to leave, Matt." At his halfhearted arguments she shook her head. "I can catch a cab."

"I'll drive you," Kennedy said.

Hayley didn't waste time arguing. She quickly headed for the door, giving a hurried smile of greeting to several businessmen who worked for one of Sin-

clair, Holmsby, and Layton's corporate accounts she
had the misfortune to meet at the door. She saw the
look of surprise that crossed their faces when they
realized the dark-haired man she was with was none
other than Kennedy Taft.

The Cheswick Hotel was connected to the underground parking structure which was also used by the
Den of Antiquity. Hayley walked silently through the
carpeted passageway, supremely conscious of the man
beside her.

"Thanks for the offer," she said, as they passed
through the deep-red-carpeted lobby to the uniformed man at the revolving door, "but I'll catch a
cab."

Outside, the cloudburst Hayley had prayed for
earlier was pouring onto the streets. November's chill
and gloom followed a man whose black coat was slick
with rain into the lobby. He shook the rain off his
umbrella onto the lush carpet.

"Who's Sheryl?" Kennedy asked soberly.

"Sheryl? Oh . . ." Hayley felt a flash of humor as
she saw the scene from Kennedy's uninformed point
of view. "She's Matt's wife. They're getting a divorce."

"She's divorcing him."

Hayley inclined her head. It was a statement, not a
question. She made a move toward the door, a
good-bye forming on her lips, when several more
people scurried inside from the rain. A blast of frigid
air preceded them. Hayley shivered.

"Since you're determined to elude me, I'll have to

say good-bye," Kennedy said. "But can I buy you a cup of coffee first? I promise to behave."

Hayley looked through the floor-to-ceiling windows beside the Cheswick's lobby doors. Rivulets of rain streaked the panes, and the doorman's breath could be seen as he paced in front of the hotel.

Hayley tried to say no, but when she turned to Kennedy a distracting softness had entered his eyes. Hayley's respect and attraction for him made it impossible for her to walk out. Knowing she was making a big mistake, she asked with a smile, "Promise?"

He held up two fingers for Scout's honor.

Hayley let him guide her up the two steps to the Cheswick's open lobby restaurant. He seemed so at ease with his surroundings that she remarked, "You've become very familiar with Portland in a short period of time. The Den, now the Cheswick . . ."

Kennedy pulled out a chair for her. "Not that familiar." His mouth curved humorously. "I'm staying at the Cheswick, Miss Sinclair. . . ."

Chapter Three

$\mathcal{K}$ennedy stared across the circular table and wondered about the series of emotions crossing Hayley Sinclair's mobile face. He'd never encountered such a woman. The dichotomy of her both intrigued and amazed him, making it possible to forget all the reasons she was "hands off" to Kennedy Taft, the director.

She was trying desperately not to appear surprised by his announcement. He could see the effort it cost her; the events of the day certainly had taken their toll. But it was painfully obvious that she was affected nonetheless, and Kennedy found himself liking the idea that it mattered to her at all.

Her gray eyes wouldn't quite meet his. She looked at his hands, at his loosened tie, at a point somewhere to the left of his ear. For all her poise in the courtroom, Hayley Sinclair was singularly uneasy with a man.

Or was it just him? Kennedy had to admit that he did represent a kind of threat to her. But considering the way things had gone in court . . . did it matter so much anymore?

Hayley glanced at her watch again, then, for a brief instant, met Kennedy's unwavering eyes. "I get the feeling you'd like to talk about something," she said. "The trial?"

"Do you?"

Hayley managed a grim smile. "No."

Kennedy deliberately held her gaze. "You didn't expect to lose, did you?"

"I'd hoped not to."

"For personal convictions?"

"And for my career." Hayley tentatively placed her lips against the steaming cup of coffee. "But I already told you that."

He watched her carefully take a sip. "Why you?" he asked suddenly.

Hayley looked up. "What do you mean?"

"Why were you picked to represent Claudia Jeffries?"

Kennedy could have no way of knowing about the conversation Hayley had had in her father's office that afternoon, yet Hayley resented him for touching such a sensitive nerve. "You flattered me earlier, Mr. Taft, but now I think you're saying what you really feel."

"I'm not implying that you were wrong for the job."

"Aren't you?" Hayley lifted her chin defiantly.

"Then how come I get that impression every time you look at me? Be honest, hasn't it crossed your mind just once that the prosecution would have been better off to have a man?"

Kennedy realized that he'd trespassed into forbidden territory. He instinctively sensed that her anger wasn't meant completely for him. "Of course it crossed my mind."

Hayley blinked in surprise at his honesty. She'd expected all kinds of excuses and placating responses.

He didn't give her time to respond before he said, "I suppose I actually hoped you were terrible; young, inexperienced, easily flustered. . . ." He gave her a swift look that assessed, and . . . desired? "Needless to say you proved me wrong."

Hayley was beginning to think she'd completely underestimated him. She chose to match his straightforwardness, sensing that she could quickly get in over her head with this man. "Why did you want to see me? Seriously. You don't need to keep complimenting me to win me over. Just say what's on your mind."

Hayley froze when his palm suddenly closed over hers. It was such an intimate, unexpected gesture.

"Do I have to want something?" he asked quickly.

"Most people do." Hayley's heart was beating heavily. Her chest felt constricted; her attention focused on the spreading warmth from his hand.

Seconds passed. Eons. Briefly, Hayley wondered what was happening to her. She was fascinated and afraid, aware that something totally foreign and out of control could overtake her if she wasn't extremely careful.

"All right, then. I do want something." Before Hayley's disappointment could register fully, he went on, "I want to see you, as a woman. Just you."

Hayley tried to drag her hand back. She jostled her cup and watched the coffee swirl in angry waves. "You've seen me," she said, trying to keep things light.

"I've seen an associate for Sinclair, Holmsby, and Layton. I don't want to see her. I want to see Hayley Sinclair."

"They're one and the same."

"Are they? Why don't I think so?"

"Mr. Taft . . ." Hayley's voice trailed off at the look on his face. He was watching her with such sheer concentration that she couldn't hide. She hated herself for all the verbal game playing she'd been doing, but how could she behave any other way?

"So far you've been incredibly honest," Kennedy said with a deliberation Hayley found frightening. "Don't blow it now. I wanted to see you because you're an interesting woman who fascinates the hell out of me. I haven't felt that way in a long, long time. Maybe never."

Hayley's mouth was dry. *How can this be happening?* She felt trouble rushing at her with the force and speed of a freight train. The touch of his hand was doing crazy, wild things to her imagination.

"You make it impossible for me to answer, Mr. Taft."

"I wish you wouldn't do that."

"Do what?" Hayley was anxious for a diversion, but wary of his amused tone.

"Keep calling me Mr. Taft. Kennedy's shorter."

"And more intimate?"

He grinned. "Something like that."

Hayley's pulse had slowed to a rhythm she could deal with. As the moment stretched between them, she dared to ask, "You were married once, weren't you?"

The question was rhetorical. She already knew more about him than most. "Yes," he answered shortly, wondering what was to come.

"So was I, Mr. Taft. It lasted eighteen months. And it was the most miserable time of my life."

Kennedy's brows blunted into a frown. He sensed her pulling out of reach in yet another way.

Hayley pondered her own reasons for revealing such an intimate detail of her life. After several moments, she said flatly, "I'm not looking for another relationship with anyone. A brief affair isn't my cup of tea."

"I'm not trying to talk you into bed."

The calm surety and simple truth in his voice caused a rush of color to stain Hayley's cheeks. "Then I'm all out of options. I don't know what you want." *Dear God,* she thought, *how did I ever get here with him?*

"I want you to relax," Kennedy said.

"I can't. Not tonight." Hayley wished she could explain herself to him, her need for solitude. Whether he realized it or not—and she was sure he did— Kennedy was infringing on the wall of resistance she'd built against the opposite sex. She didn't have time for, and wasn't interested in, the kind of brief affair he could give. Maybe he wasn't trying to talk her into bed, but he was slowly gaining a foothold on the slippery wall of her resistance.

"I've got to go." Hayley stood up abruptly, relieved to pull her hand from the imprisonment of his.

This time he made no effort to stop her. He rose beside her, his expression thoughtful. Hayley had already forgotten how much taller he was than she. She felt overwhelmed and unaccountably depressed by the way the whole ruinous day had turned out.

"I'll take you home," he said again.

"No, really. Thank you, but I can catch a cab."

"Let me, Hayley. I want to."

She shook her head mutely, a kind of negative acquiescence that Kennedy either understood or simply disregarded. She followed him back to the parking lot, to the rented Lincoln Continental that looked as if it had never before been used.

The silence between them was only interrupted when Hayley had to offer directions to her apartment. Rain ran down the windshield, to be swept away by the steady wipers. Inside, the smell of leather and male cologne enveloped Hayley in nostalgic memories she hadn't known she possessed. She looked out the window. She'd never felt this way with a man before.

Hayley lived in the West Hills, an older, prestigious part of Portland, where she'd grown up. As Kennedy's car nosed up the narrow, switchback roads, Hayley tried to empty her mind of all thought. She closed her eyes briefly, then snapped them open as she felt a burning intrigue, a latent hunger, somehow invade her body.

"It's right up on the left. There's an old house that's

been converted to apartments. You can let me out on the stairway below."

He parked the car. "I'll walk you up."

Hayley didn't argue. She'd learned enough about him during the last few hours to know it wouldn't work anyway.

The stairs were rough-cut stones, hemmed by lush banks of ivy. In the dark, Hayley balanced her umbrella and cautiously mounted the slippery steps. An outdoor lamppost was the only salvation for the treacherous path.

Hayley's apartment was on the bottom floor. Her hands were numb with cold as she tried to insert the key in the lock. It wouldn't turn. "Oh, God," she moaned in despair, staring at her frozen fingers as if they were the enemy.

In a gesture of pure arrogant masculinity, Kennedy took the keys from her and worked to open the stubborn door. It gave with a groan of reluctance, and Hayley skimmed inside.

"Thank you . . . for everything," she said, watching rain pour off his hair onto the lapels of his coat. The shoulders of his suede jacket were stained with water. Hayley was sure it was ruined.

She hoped he would just leave and not make her look like an idiot, hanging by the door. All she wanted now was to be left alone.

Guilt at her own rudeness ravaged her brain. She stared at him in abashment. How could she be acting this way, when all he'd been was nice to her? Feeling as though she was burning her last bridge, Hayley heard herself ask, "Would you like to come in for a minute? I know it's pouring, and I've been . . ." Hayley backed away from the door, letting her words trail off uncertainly. She'd been terribly rude.

Kennedy hesitated fractionally, then moved with sudden decision. He shut the door and ran a hand through his wet hair. There was something elemental in that simple gesture that made Hayley wished she'd listened to her instincts.

"And here I was sure you wouldn't ask me in," he murmured in gentle rebuke.

She was beginning to think she couldn't deny him anything. "Would you like a drink?" she asked, moving toward the kitchen. His sure steps followed behind her.

Hayley's kitchen was a small **U**. Kennedy stood in the doorway, leaning his shoulder against the jamb, watching her search through her cupboards with amusement.

"All I have is champagne. Bought on sale, and it wasn't expensive to begin with."

The edges of his eyes crinkled into a fine web. "How about coffee?"

"Instant?"

"Is there any other kind?"

Hayley made them each a cup, then turned, holding the steaming mugs gingerly. Kennedy reached for her outstretched offering, his palms carefully taking the cup from hers, fingers brushing briefly. He stepped aside, allowing her just enough space to get by.

The apartment had hardwood floors covered by

luxurious woven rugs. Hayley knelt in front of the marble fireplace, its eggshell white molding and tiered mantel elegantly stating the beauty of a bygone era.

Kennedy was there before she tossed the first log on. Not giving her time to protest, he said, "Let me. I've already ruined my clothes anyway, whereas you're still as beautiful as you were in the courtroom."

Hayley automatically glanced at her clothes. A different suit, but the same look. In no way would she consider herself beautiful.

He was already expertly stacking the wood on the fire, and Hayley watched. She could see the strength that bunched in his shoulders, and imagined the fluid muscles that worked beneath.

"Don't you Californians know how to dress for rain?" she couldn't resist asking, needing something —anything—to say.

"Ahh, shucks, ma'am. I'm from New Mexico. Folks there never learned to dress for rain neither."

Hayley's mouth twitched into a smile. "Sorry."

Kennedy leaned back on one heel. The flames curled eagerly around the dry alder. Pungent, woodsy smoke drafted up the chimney, and the aroma and sound of bubbling resin filled the room. "You should be," he told her with mock severity. "You Oregonians are so territorial. My God, California's your neighbor, not the outer limits."

Hayley tried to relax. After a few more moments of watching Kennedy's back, she deliberately kicked off her shoes and curled her feet beneath her on the couch—what she would normally do if she were alone. She cupped her coffee, and asked, "What about Hollywood? It's been said you need a passport to enter."

The almost imperceptible stiffening of his shoulders made Hayley regret the jab. After all, Hollywood was his home. He was a famous director, a master of his art. And that art had brought him to Portland to clash with Hayley Sinclair.

"You disdain what I do, don't you?"

Startled, Hayley's eyes widened. His face was half-averted from her, his body delicately poised on one foot, completely still.

"Why . . . no. I don't *disdain* it." She hadn't meant to come off sounding superior.

His head turned, silver-green eyes driving into hers. "But it's frivolous. A waste of time. And dangerous—to the people who actually work to put that fantasy on film."

Hayley set her cup down carefully. Had she been attacking? Or was the issue simply something neither of them could avoid? "It was dangerous for Carl Jeffries," she said evenly. "It's undoubtedly dangerous for others."

"Lots of jobs are dangerous. What you really object to is the fact that the 'danger' is so needless, don't you? To you it's an unnecessary risk."

Hayley started to protest, then stopped. He was absolutely right, and why that should bother her she had no earthly idea. But it did.

Kennedy poked the end of a log and sparks flew

furiously up the chimney. He replaced the poker, then
turned his back to the fire, studying Hayley. "I hate
myself for what happened to Carl," he said.

Shock widened Hayley's eyes. "You blame yourself," she said on an ascending note, realizing how
very damaging his words were, what they could have
meant to her case against him.

"No. Not the way you mean. Some things are
unavoidable no matter what you do."

"You mean, fate?" Hayley asked dryly.

"If you like." Heat filled the room, and with a
distracted gesture Kennedy jerked on his tie. He
undid his top shirt button, and crisp, dark hair was
revealed at the open neckline. "There are such things
as safety standards in the film industry, Hayley. You
know that. But people have to enforce them."

"People like you?"

Kennedy held her antagonistic gaze. "Yes. And
people like Bill Baines, the man who let Carl on that
boat. *And people like Carl Jeffries.*" He pulled off his
jacket and flung it into the only vacant chair. Then,
after a moment of hesitation, he walked to the other
end of the couch and sat next to Hayley.

Hayley's spine was painfully straight. She wasn't
sure what was happening although she had the strange
feeling she shouldn't be any part of it. But what did it
matter? She wasn't involved with the Taft case anymore. Yet, crazily, she didn't want to hear any more.
She didn't want to *know*.

"Jeffries should have known his own ability, Hayley," Kennedy maintained. "The Clackamas is no
river for an amateur. And he shouldn't have been

there anyway." His hand moved impatiently, then he ran it around the back of his neck. "That's where the holes were in your case. I had no control over Jeffries. He wasn't even supposed to be there."

"You were the director."

"Right. But I'm not another man's keeper."

He was staring at her with those watchful eyes. For some reason, she felt she had to defend herself. "Maybe not," she agreed. "But then, somewhere, somehow, something's got to change. That accident shouldn't have happened, for whatever the reason."

Kennedy let out a long breath. "You were trying to set a precedent."

Hayley nearly winced. That sounded so cold-blooded when equated with destroying a man's career. "It takes that sometimes, Mr. Taft."

"I'm not arguing—"

"Why aren't you?" Hayley's demand slipped out before she could think. "Why *aren't* you? If someone tried to sue me and I felt I was innocent, I'd be furious. I can't believe you're that forgiving."

"It's not a matter of forgiveness."

Hayley shook her head, releasing errant strands of honey gold hair from her loose chignon. They fell unheeded against her neck, and she impatiently brushed them back.

"I've been sued before, you know that," he said.

Yes, Hayley knew. She knew all kinds of facts about Kennedy Taft. And she knew the suit that had been against him before was settled out of court. An actress had claimed he'd purposely ruined her performance, then subsequently fired her from the film. The settlement had been small and, Hayley felt, had been given simply to avoid the costs of a trial. Kennedy had been adamantly against it.

"I'm just surprised at your complacency, that's all. Most people take a suit very personally."

His gaze dropped over her, in a suddenly intimate, blatantly desirous way. "You think I should resent you?" he asked.

"It would be perfectly natural."

"Well." Hayley froze as he lightly brushed back a tempting strand of hair, sending a shiver along her nape. "I don't."

Hayley's breath was trapped in her throat. "I get the feeling I've already said more to you than I should have. I'll regret it tomorrow." She tried to ease herself away.

"There's nothing to regret. The trial's over."

"Claudia's hoping to appeal."

"But you aren't the prosecuting lawyer."

Hayley's smile held a trace of bitterness. "You're remarkably well informed. What if Claudia Jeffries should change her mind?"

His lashes lowered; his glance was deceptively lazy as he said, "I still won't believe I've made a mistake, Lady Prosecutor. You've got incredible integrity, and even more incredible legs."

Hayley immediately swung her legs to the floor, her skirt daringly hiked intriguing inches above her knee. Kennedy's satisfied chuckle made her furious with herself.

"Why are you so afraid of me?" he asked.

"I'm not."

"What the hell do you call this? The body language is pretty clear."

Hayley's arms were crossed beneath her breasts, her knees clamped so tightly she could have been holding a dime between them. Knowing she was being ridiculous, she couldn't seem to act naturally.

"Mr. Taft . . ."

"Do you want me to leave?"

Yes! No. Hayley could only shake her head at the impossibilities ravaging her own mind. She dared a glance at him; he was waiting, poised, for the rejection.

It was his patient acceptance of whatever her decision would be that was Hayley's undoing. "I have no idea in the world what I want." She sighed. "You . . . you're . . ." She drew a calming breath. "This day has made me crazy. But whatever you think, I'm not afraid of you. I'm just cautious."

He looked at her thoughtfully. "Because of who I am? Or because of your ex-husband?"

Hayley took another deep breath. "Probably a little of both."

"And if I weren't Kennedy Taft, the director, the *defendant.*" He stressed the word with soft mockery. "What then?"

"Then you'd just be a man who lived in another state."

To her surprise, he chuckled. "Oh, Hayley, it's not that far away."

He was outmaneuvering her. Hayley's courtroom

instincts warned her that he was—in his own very
effective way—trying to close off each of her arguments.

"I don't want an affair, Kennedy," she said suc-
cinctly.

Her use of his first name, coupled with her determined tone, was an intriguing aggravation that made
Kennedy swear softly beneath his breath. "Don't
want, or don't have time for?" he asked harshly.

He read her far too accurately. "Don't want," she
stated flatly.

She should have seen the challenge coming. Later,
she even asked herself if, subconsciously, she'd deliberately delivered it. But when Kennedy suddenly
shifted, placing his hands on her shoulders, Hayley's
lips parted in disbelief.

Very slowly, giving her ample time to elude him,
Kennedy tucked his finger beneath her chin, turning
her face to meet the determination of his. There was a
grimness to the slant of his jaw that said any halfhearted excuses would be ignored. Hayley stared into
the silvery glints of steel in his eyes, her heart
thudding.

"What if I said I don't believe you?" he said softly,
his lips a hairsbreadth from hers.

Before she could answer, his mouth met hers.
Hayley's immobility was partly shock, partly a kind of
frozen anticipation.

She wanted to kiss him, wanted him to kiss her. Her
reservations weren't so intense as to deny herself that
simple pleasure. But when his lips met hers, gently
touching, searching, then growing greedily bolder,

Hayley was totally unprepared for the storm of responses that ripped through her.

His arms tightened around her, pressing her breasts against the hard muscles of his chest. Blood pounding, Hayley felt starved for air but totally incapable of pulling back from the gentle mastery of his mouth.

His tongue touched her teeth, and Hayley's lips parted further, almost dazedly. *This can't be happening,* she thought even as she yearned to be closer, as close to him as she could possibly be. She was amazed that her mind even worked that way.

"I . . . can't . . . ," she tried to say.

"Shhh."

"No, it's not you. It's . . . everything."

His hand had found the small of her back, and was dragging her closer, the only sounds the rustling of her skirt against the stiff material of the couch and the restless movements of his caressing fingers. She felt them on her back, down her spine, at her waist. Heat was swallowing her up inside. Her own hands were gripped tightly to the hard swell of his upper arms, the tension within him almost shocking.

She moved her mouth from the torment of his, offering him the soft skin of her neck. It was an unknowing move, and when she felt the pressure of his lips, the sensual touch of his tongue, she quivered with a mixture of desire and premonition.

"Wait. I can't . . ."

His teeth found the soft lobe of one ear. Hayley heard his breath magnified and her pulse pounded like a savage surf.

"Can't what?" he murmured, his mouth traveling a dangerous path back to hers.

"Kennedy . . ."

He pressed kisses to the corners of her mouth until she could no longer hide her shudders of desire. Hayley knew she was lost; she had no defense. He felt her submission instantly, his mouth urgently moving against her lips, one hand caught in the tangled tresses from her fallen chignon.

"Love, oh love," he murmured, caught by the same hunger that had entrapped Hayley. A dark ache enveloped him, so huge and unexpected that Kennedy forgot anything but the very moment.

His hand slid convulsively up and down her spine, pulling her so tightly against him that she could feel the heavy pounding of his heart. How things had gotten so out of control so quickly, Hayley didn't have time to consider. Emotions she hadn't known still existed poured through her with exhausting intensity. Her breath was ragged. So was Kennedy's. Buttons were coming free, and when his hand curved around her breast, Hayley strained against him instinctively. Thought, regret, shame . . . none of that entered her head.

"Hayley . . ." His voice was unsteady. She kissed his lips, tentatively, exploring him in a dreamlike state. Then he filled his palms with the soft swell of her hips and she was lifted against his hardness with urgent need.

The shock of such rapid, blatant intimacy was a cold shower of sanity. Hayley's eyes flew open. She took a huge gulp of air and said in a strangled voice, "My

God . . . I never meant . . ." Her head snapped back, hands pushing on his shoulders. "Things cannot go this *far!*" she blurted.

It took Kennedy a few moments to realize she was struggling in earnest. His body was slower to switch gears than Hayley's. She was pulling herself from his arms before the rage of adrenaline and desire had cooled inside him.

His mind was clear enough, however, to recognize that their brief and explosive lovemaking was over. With a slow release of breath he raked a trembling hand through his hair and tried not to notice the swelling curve and rigid nipples of Hayley's breasts through the sheer bra, which was now exposed.

Hayley jerked the two halves of her blouse together. "I'm sorry," she was saying disjointedly. "I'm sorry." She knew how ridiculous she sounded but couldn't help herself. "I never wanted to—never meant to—"

He let her talk because he didn't trust himself to speak yet. Hayley turned her palms up in a beseeching gesture, her eyes a confused dove gray. "I'm just not ready. . . ."

Her honesty hadn't deserted her. He knew exactly what she meant. And after experiencing the incredible passion that existed between them, he wasn't sure he was ready either.

He traced the curve of her cheekbone with his thumb. "It's all right, love," he said huskily. "I wasn't exactly prepared myself."

As her senses fully returned, Hayley could scarcely believe he wasn't furious with her. She knew how far passion had taken them, and she was aware that her abrupt turnaround was far more difficult on him than on herself.

She tried buttoning her blouse, but was unable to with his eyes on her—deceptively hidden by his lashes or no. She stood up, tried to think of something to say, then walked rather unsteadily toward the kitchen.

A few minutes later he was standing in the doorway.

Hayley shrugged her shoulders, trying desperately to treat the situation with sophistication. She hadn't realized how sorely she lacked experience in the dating game until now. "I don't know what to say. I'm sorry. I . . ."

She shushed instantly when he raised his hand. "Forget it," he said lightly. "There's nothing to be sorry about. I'll live." His mouth twisted charmingly. "Maybe."

"I didn't mean to give the impression that I say one thing and mean another," she said on a shaky laugh.

"You didn't. Look." Kennedy came a few steps closer and Hayley turned a wide open face to his. *She has no idea how vulnerable she looks,* Kennedy thought, aware of a need growing inside him. "Maybe I'm moving too fast for you. Like you said, it's been a crazy day. But I don't want to stop now."

He paused, and Hayley's imagination ran rampant, wondering what was coming next. She was totally unprepared.

"I want you to come to California with me."

Her mouth dropped. "What?"

"Just for a visit," he said with a smile. "To show you we Hollywood types aren't all bad."

He was going way too fast. "Now?" she questioned.

"Whenever you like."

The dismissive gesture of his shoulders did nothing to reassure Hayley. "I can't. I couldn't . . . my schedule. . . ." She paused to collect herself.

He sensed she was about to close the door permanently. With a quick movement, he held her shoulders lightly in his grasp; her gray eyes widened at the sudden contact. "Think about it. My time here's running out and I don't want to lose you before I even have a chance to win."

"Why does it matter so much?" she asked.

He kissed her briefly, warmly. "I don't know. But it matters to you, too, doesn't it?"

Hayley nodded, half-dazed. It had mattered from the moment she'd first laid eyes on him. Why, she had no answer. But she couldn't shake the feeling that she was tempting fate just by being with him.

She let him pull her into his arms once more, with a tenderness that had nothing to do with passion. He stroked her hair, and kissed her forehead; then he stood back, looking at her for a long moment before he tugged her hand, walking with her to the door.

"I'll call you tomorrow," he said, and Hayley nodded mutely.

When he was gone she stared at the door, bemused. *I'm falling in love with you,* she thought with a tiny shock.

Chapter Four

"You and I need to talk," Hayley said sternly, as she walked into Matthew's office the next morning, balancing two cups of coffee. She handed him one, and he raised his brows in surprise.

"What did I do to deserve this?" he asked.

Hayley glared at him in mock severity. "Absolutely nothing. In fact, the way I see things, you owe me an apology. Just where do you get off abandoning me to Kennedy Taft?" she demanded. "Thanks a whole bunch."

The corners of Matthew's mouth turned up in the semblance of a smile. He looked—Hayley noticed belatedly—terrible, as if he'd come straight to work without going to bed at all. "Sorry, Hayley," he said, sighing. "Sheryl called and things just happened. . . ." His voice trailed off on a peculiar note of resignation. He seemed to realize how he sounded and his spine straightened involuntarily. A sly smile creeping across his lips, he asked, "Was it so terrible?"

"Catastrophic. I may never recover."

Reflecting that her words were abysmally true, Hayley tried to forget her startling emotions of the night before and concentrate on Matt. Not an easy task, considering she was still reeling from her explosive and totally unexpected reaction to Kennedy's lovemaking.

"Everything okay with you?" she asked Matt carefully, sensing his precarious mood.

Matthew's smile dropped. "What does that mean?"

"It means that I'm concerned about you, friend. That's all."

He flexed his shoulders wearily, stifling a yawn with a sip from his coffee cup. "Sorry," he muttered vaguely.

Unsure of how to proceed, but remembering why he'd left her to her own fate the night before, Hayley struck at the issue that had to be foremost on his mind. "How did it go last night with Sheryl?"

Matt's face darkened. For a minute Hayley thought he was going to tell her to mind her own business, but after a weighty pause, he said, "Oh, fine . . . nothing much happened."

Hayley didn't argue the point, though Matthew's evident tiredness said he'd either stayed up late, or spent a sleepless night. Either way, she was certain Sheryl had a lot to do with it.

"Are you seeing her again?" Hayley asked, sipping from her cup.

"I don't know." He gave her an impatient stare. "Am I on trial here? Or, are you just getting even over last night?"

"I'm getting even over last night," Hayley answered lightly, sorry she'd brought the subject up.

Matt's aggressiveness disappeared as quickly as it had arisen. He opened his mouth to say something, then closed it. After a minute, he said on a heartfelt sigh, "Let's not talk about Sheryl, okay?"

"Sure." Hayley had the distinct impression that things had gone poorly between Matthew and his soon-to-be ex-wife. She was more than relieved to change the subject.

"So, how was your evening with Taft?" Matthew asked unexpectedly.

Hayley narrowed her eyes at him. "Surprisingly good, no thanks to you."

"He likes you. I can tell."

Hayley lowered her eyes to her coffee cup, growing uneasy at the turnabout. "He's an interesting man," she said noncommittally.

The laugh that erupted from Matthew had an element in it that Hayley didn't like. It was too knowing, too smug. "I feel a romance brewing," he said wickedly.

Hayley made an exasperated sound. "Your imagination's working overtime. I'm not in the market for romance."

"But Taft is. Too bad we didn't realize it earlier. It might have helped Claudia Jeffries's case."

"I hope you're kidding," Hayley returned a trifle dryly. There was no way in the world she would have tried to use Kennedy to further Claudia Jeffries's case against him—even if she'd been able to. Professional ethics were involved. But Matt seemed to be half-serious. She gave him an uneasy stare and wondered if she was being too sensitive about Kennedy, about the whole Taft case in general.

"Oh, Hayley . . ." Matthew's hand went over his heart. "You wound me," he said theatrically.

Hayley was relieved and glad to get away from discussing Kennedy. "You're such a ham," she accused, and Matthew finally laughed.

"Did you just get to work?" Matthew's eyes caught the glint of raindrops still in her hair, and Hayley nodded.

"An accident backed up traffic for twenty minutes, and I'm lucky to be here so soon. Good thing I didn't have any appointments this morning."

Matthew regarded her consideringly. "Then you haven't heard the news."

"What news?" Hayley's brows drew into a frown. Matthew's tone boded trouble.

"Claudia Jeffries has already gotten a new attorney. The incomparable Warren Smythe."

Matt made a sweeping, spiteful gesture with his hand, but Hayley barely noticed. Inside, she felt oddly upset. Warren Smythe was a forceful, arrogant and heavy-handed attorney who—in Hayley's opinion—always tried to bully a jury to his way of thinking. His tactics were in direct opposition to Hayley's, and though she understood Claudia Jeffries's rationale—

the woman wanted someone as different from Hayley as she could find—her pride was still wounded by Claudia's deliberate choice.

"Warren Smythe will do a good job for her," Hayley admitted with forced graciousness.

"Are you serious?" Matt was incredulous. "He'll bulldoze his way through an appeal. If he gets a new trial, the jury won't know what hit them."

"Maybe that's not so bad," Hayley said quietly. "I get the feeling Smythe is the kind of attorney Claudia needs."

Matthew glowered. "But you're the kind of attorney Lisa Jeffries needs, Hayley."

Hayley sat down in one of the blue-cushioned, bleached-oak chairs. That was the problem, of course; the nag in the back of her mind. Lisa Jeffries deserved decent representation, but also compassion. Hayley had tried to minimize the poor girl's exposure to the public eye, but a trial with Warren Smythe prosecuting would hurl her brutally onto the front page again. Neither Warren nor Claudia would probably even consider the effect it would have on Lisa.

"Well, it's out of my hands," Hayley murmured. "Maybe Claudia's more sensitive to her daughter's needs than we know."

Matthew snorted. "Yeah, sure . . ."

Hayley left Matthew's office feeling vaguely disquieted. She tried to put the whole thing behind her, but it followed her around, making her feel as if there should have been more she could have done. She felt—though at this juncture it was a moot issue—that Lisa Jeffries hadn't gotten the fairness she deserved.

And Kennedy Taft?

Hayley's fine brows pulled together. Guiltily, she knew that even if she could have helped Lisa, she was relieved that she wouldn't have to battle Kennedy in court again. She simply wouldn't have been able to. Her emotions were in such an uproar over him that her judgment was affected.

Having Warren Smythe become Claudia's new attorney was best all the way around, she concluded sternly as she pushed open the door to her office. *It's time to forget all about it—him—and get on with something else!*

But as she reached for her appointment book, a pair of silvery green eyes swam across her inner vision.

I want you to come to California with me. . . .

Hayley's flesh quivered as her thoughts touched on the night before. She was half-terrified, half-fascinated, by the feelings that churned within her just by remembering. There was something urgent and elemental about Kennedy that took her breath away. The mobile velvet of his lips, the shock of steel muscles, his incredibly sensuous touch . . . Hayley closed her eyes and shuddered, feeling warmth flood over her even now. What was happening to her? She was old enough to know better.

Or was she?

The appointments blurred in front of her. She thought about the work scheduled for her in the next few weeks, picking out what was most important, most pressing. There were only one or two things. . . .

Good Lord! Hayley gasped in dismay. She was actually considering Kennedy's invitation!

With a sound of frustration, directed solely at herself, Hayley slammed the appointment book shut. Moments later a sheepish smile crossed her face as she considered that silly, impulsive move.

"Face it, counselor," she murmured to herself. "This is *your* problem. And the only way to reconcile it, is to recognize it first."

She tried unsuccessfully to do just that for most of the morning. By lunchtime, she was no nearer to putting her feelings in perspective than she'd been earlier. Shaking her honey blond mane in exasperation, she grabbed her raincoat and hurried to meet her father for lunch.

"Tom Wilson, the Computektron employee, is waiting to talk to you," Jason Sinclair said on the walk back from the restaurant.

The skies were overcast and dreary. Hayley blinked in surprise, staring at her father through the filmy drizzle of rain. "Me? But that's Matthew's case."

"Maybe not," he said cryptically, holding the door to the lobby for her. Hayley stepped inside, folding her umbrella, smiling at the uniformed lobby attendant standing guard.

She followed her father to the bank of elevators, and remained silent beside him on the swift ride up to their offices. She was disturbed by her father's revelations, but knew him well enough to realize he usually had very good reasons for his decisions.

Tom Wilson was a tall, slim man in his late thirties or early forties. He wore steel-rimmed glasses and a serious expression. As Hayley entered her father's office, his eyes scanned her dispassionately, and he said, as a way of greeting, "I saw you on television."

Hayley managed a smile. Knowing how damaging that film clip had been to her professionalism, she had no idea how to respond.

"Tom's filing a reverse-discrimination suit," Jason Sinclair enlightened Hayley. "Computektron denied him a promotion he highly deserved in favor of a younger, inexperienced woman. The woman's twenty-four years old, and has been with the company less than a year. She does, however, have a master's degree, something Tom doesn't, but Tom has fifteen years' experience."

"She's sleeping with the boss," Tom declared flatly.

Hayley felt like she'd arrived at a play during the second act. Foremost in her mind was why she was being considered for the case. It had already been given to Matthew and she didn't want to start ill feelings floating through the offices.

And, beyond all that, she wasn't terribly impressed with Tom Wilson's attitude.

Forcing a neutral tone, she said, "This woman's personal relationship with her employer won't be an issue if, and when, we go to trial. The case has got to be tried pitting your credentials against hers—period."

Hayley was aware she sounded as if she were delivering an ultimatum, and perhaps, in a way she was. But no matter who ended up trying the case, Tom Wilson needed to understand the rules of the game.

Wilson's eyes widened. "But that's the crux of the problem!" he sputtered. "That's why she got the promotion!"

"You don't know that," Hayley returned. "And bringing it up in court won't work. It's hearsay. Believe me, Mr. Wilson," she added with a trace of bitterness, "the jury will probably come to the same conclusion you have, anyway."

A strained silence filled the room. Hayley had no wish to alienate a potential client, but she'd heard that old "sleeping with the boss" line too many times. Her sensitivity, she supposed, was magnified where Tom Wilson was concerned, because she was aware that he'd seen her folly with Kennedy Taft on television.

Hayley's father cleared his throat. "Well, I think the ground rules have been established," he said, his tone laced with irony.

Hayley looked at Tom Wilson. Computektron was a nationally renowned, locally headquartered electronics firm, and anyone connected with the lawsuit would undoubtedly be afforded some publicity. She wasn't certain she was ready to be that person—especially so soon after the Taft trial, and she knew it wasn't worth alienating Matthew unless Tom Wilson understood and agreed with her way of thinking.

Tom Wilson was staring right back at her. Whatever else she'd done, she'd gotten his attention. He seemed to consider for a few moments, then said, "I'll be blunt with you, Miss Sinclair. I didn't agree with your father's advice to use you as my attorney."

He stopped, his brows drawn into a tense line, and Hayley knew what he was thinking. The boss's daughter. She'd been turned down because of her connection with her father more than once.

"But he thought it would be good to have a woman on my side," Tom went on, "given the situation."

Hayley glanced sharply at her father. He was a crafty devil, that was for sure. Having Tom Wilson's lawyer be a woman would curb any speculation that the man was simply jealous and bitter against the female population as a whole.

"So you're saying you've changed your mind?" Jason Sinclair asked him.

Tom Wilson smiled, lessening his rigid, schoolmaster expression. "Yes," he said.

A weighty discussion on all the particulars of the case ensued. Hayley pushed her worries over usurping one of Matthew's clients to the back of her mind, knowing the decision had been her father's, and therefore out of both her and Matthew's control. She'd been selected to be Tom Wilson's legal representation, and she intended to give it her best effort. But even as she worked out some of the key issues with Tom, she was determined to catch Matthew alone as soon as possible and explain just exactly what had happened.

Late in the afternoon, the receptionist buzzed Jason Sinclair's office. "There's a phone call for Hayley," her voice said across the interoffice speaker.

Hayley's father looked impatient. "Can't it wait?"

"He says it's urgent." A long pause followed. "The caller is Mr. Kennedy Taft."

Hayley felt her face flush a deep, revealing red. She straightened involuntarily, meeting her father's quizzical eyes.

"What does he want?" he asked her.

"I don't know." Hayley rose stiffly, aware that she wasn't being entirely truthful. "I'll find out and let you know."

She felt her father's and Tom Wilson's interested eyes on her back as she headed for the door. She closed it with a soft click behind her, letting out a pent-up breath, feeling oddly as if the moment of truth had come.

How had things gotten so out of control? Hayley felt ridiculously like a traitor, as if by merely speaking with Kennedy Taft she was betraying a confidence.

The light on her phone was blinking, and when she saw the raft of "while you were out" messages on her desk—all from Kennedy—Hayley understood why his call had been labeled urgent. He was tired of waiting.

She counted to five before she picked up the receiver, consciously willing her heartbeat to settle down. Her reaction was way out of line to the circumstances.

"Hayley Sinclair," she answered in a neutral tone. Out of the blue, before he even uttered a word, she remembered her thought of the night before. *I'm falling in love with you.*

She blinked rapidly, sinking into her chair as Kennedy's voice drawled across the line, "Has anyone ever told you that it's hell getting through to you?"

His voice was warm and rich and full of waiting promises. Hayley let her gaze slip to the impressionistic painting in tones of gray and aqua that hung on the far side of the room. She needed something cool and remote to keep herself hanging on the brink of sanity.

"Many times," she said, congratulating herself on her poise. "I've been accused of being stubborn, persistent and even deliberately obtuse. It's also hard to reach me at the office," she added in mock confidence.

He laughed in pure enjoyment, a sound that sent a chill of pleasure up Hayley's arms. "You're too busy for your own good," he accused softly.

"I like to be busy."

"I want to see you tonight."

Warnings flashed through her head. He was relentlessly stalking her, pushing her, but masking it all with a tender charm that Hayley had no defense against. "I thought you were leaving," she said, searching her mind for an excuse to say no, knowing she wouldn't find one.

Kennedy inhaled slowly, as if he, too, was fighting the breakneck pace of their relationship. "I couldn't leave without seeing you again," he said simply. "Have dinner with me."

The words echoed through Hayley's mind, nothing unusual in themselves—but the *tone*. His unconscious sensuality gave a simple invitation new meaning. Or was that just what she wanted to believe?

"Ah . . . Kennedy . . . I don't think I can." Hayley twisted the cord around one finger and desperately sought for some believable excuse.

"Why not?"

Hayley shook her head, baffled by her own responses. "I don't know yet. Give me time to think."

She heard his silent laughter. "I'll tell you what," he said outrageously, "you keep thinking, and in the meantime I'll drive to your office and pick you up."

"No . . . I can't."

"Hayley . . ."

She squeezed her eyes closed. "Look, Kennedy, the timing's all wrong. I don't know if I can adequately explain what I mean, but—"

"Is tomorrow night better?"

"No." He was flustering her—*calculatedly* flustering her.

"When, Hayley?"

Hayley bit into her lip with a vengeance. *How would you feel about maybe never, Kennedy?* "My schedule's pretty tight," she lied adroitly, making noises of flipping through her calendar. "What about lunch—sometime—maybe . . . tomorrow?"

His silence could have meant anything: irritation, frustration, determination. But when he spoke, it was with a kind of bittersweet understanding, almost resignation. "My schedule's tight, too, Hayley. I don't have very much time at all. But what I do have, I'd like to spend with you."

Hayley felt her throat close in on itself. She was no good at this sort of thing. Her breath came out in a painful little "Oh," and she knew the inevitable had caught up with her.

"Dinner?" Hayley asked, licking her dry lips.

"Whenever you can make it, love."

He had to know what her answer would be; he could see right into her soul. "How about tonight," she said in a small voice, expecting him to laugh at the way she'd tried to stall him.

But instead he merely said, "Perfect," satisfaction and relief in his voice.

"I think it would be better if you didn't come to the office. Could you pick me up at my apartment?"

Hayley didn't know what to expect. She thought he might object, or at least accuse her of being overly cautious. But he agreed with her suggestion, and soon Hayley had slipped the receiver back into its cradle, feeling slightly off-balance.

What are you afraid of? she asked herself. Kennedy Taft, the director, the *defendant?* That hardly made sense now. No, she was more concerned about Kennedy Taft, the man, and how he was upsetting the careful balance of her life.

Hayley had never thought of herself as compulsive about her lifestyle; she'd been known to be spontaneous when the occasion arose. But she had to admit to a certain complacency and unwillingness to upset the balance. After all, eighteen months of being married to Gerald had caused more than enough trauma to her system.

Gerald had long since moved on to greener pastures, but Hayley hadn't forgotten how brutally her emotions had been ripped apart. She was afraid of giving too much of herself again. And she sensed it could happen with Kennedy.

Trying not to worry herself needlessly about the future, she dialed Matthew's extension. The phone rang and rang but he didn't answer. So much for setting things straight, she thought grimly.

Halfway to Matthew's office, she met one of the secretaries. "Have you seen Matt around?" Hayley asked.

The woman shook her head. "No. I think he's gone home for the day. He looked beat."

"I guess I'll have to catch him tomorrow," Hayley murmured, wishing she could take care of the situation now, before Matthew heard about it through the grapevine. She thought of leaving him a note, but the Wilson case was something she was going to have to discuss with him face-to-face.

On the way home she tried once again to put her feelings in perspective. She was a rational woman, not used to blowing things out of proportion. *But isn't that what you've done?* she asked herself. *Blown everything out of proportion?*

The phone was ringing when she walked in the door. She knew without a doubt that it was Kennedy.

Shaking the rain from her coat, she snatched up the receiver. All of her instincts warned her against getting involved, yet she couldn't seem to leave well enough alone. A traitorous part of her was filling with excitement.

"Hello?" Her umbrella slid from her hand, as did

the file with the Computektron data. She ignored them both.

"You're home." Kennedy's low-timbred voice brought all her ambivalent feelings bubbling to the surface. "I'm on my way."

There was something so natural about the conversation, so comfortable, so *right,* that Hayley found it hard to believe there was anything unusual in it. They could have been long-ago lovers, or a happily married couple, or close friends who had grown accustomed to one another over the years. But the last thing they seemed like were two people who'd just met, a man and a woman caught in the joy of discovery.

"Kennedy?"

Hayley hadn't known what she wanted to say, but it was too late anyway. He'd already hung up.

On his way.

She dropped the receiver into its cradle, fingers covering her mouth. No, no, no! She wasn't ready for this! Any of it!

A flash of movement reflected in the mirror by the door caught her attention: it was the violent shaking of her own head.

She stared at her reflection, wondering at the sight of wide, uncertain eyes, tight lips and limp, rain-darkened hair. Her inertia turned to action, and she practically ran to the bedroom, stripping off her clothes, then turning on the taps to her shower. A smile of self-mockery followed her: she could pretend her relationship with Kennedy couldn't matter, but if she was really going on a date with him . . . well . . .

Hayley thrust her face into the hot spray of the shower. *You're crazy,* she told herself. *Deluding yourself. Mad!*

But it was an intoxicating kind of madness, a kind Hayley was incapable of fighting. Feminine pride won out over plain common sense, and she vowed she was going to look her best for him and damn the consequences.

Chapter Five

The Woodsman's Inn was a restaurant known for both its cuisine and atmosphere, an old tudor mansion that had been renovated and redecorated a half a dozen times. It was elegantly perched on a cliff above the Willamette; its site, a strategic bend of the gently flowing river. Leaded-glass windows swept the entire north side of the building, and the view on a clear day was several miles upriver. The tops of Portland's downtown skyscrapers were visible if the weather conditions were right.

But not tonight.

Tonight, Hayley could barely make out the river at all. Only the lights from the houseboats, fuzzy yellow blurs through the thin fog, illuminated the dark, moving waters.

It had been her idea to come to the restaurant;

Kennedy was a traveler in a foreign land when it came to Portland. But now she wished she'd picked somewhere a little less romantic, somewhere chic and sophisticated and full of odd-looking patrons. The Woodsman's Inn smelled of scented candles, burning pitch and pine and a musky, outdoorsy odor that she belatedly recognized as Kennedy's cologne. The setting was designed for intimacy.

Hayley's breath misted the diamond-paned window but she didn't turn away. She needed a few minutes to think in silence; she was already too attuned to her companion.

Most of the other occupants had requested tables near the floor-to-ceiling cavern of the Inn's magnificent bluestone fireplace, but Kennedy and Hayley had been seated in a quiet, secluded corner. The maître d', Hayley decided ruefully, was too sensitive by half.

"You're right again," Kennedy said, picking up the leather-covered wine list.

Hayley turned her head slowly, wondering what she'd missed.

"About the restaurant," he answered with a smile that said he understood exactly what she was feeling.

How could he? How could two people with such different backgrounds and ideals be so aware of one another's feelings?

She had to dispel this romantic mood before something she didn't want to happen, happened. "The Inn is one of Portland's best." Immediately she looked away again. She was repeating herself. And no wonder. The strong, tan column of Kennedy's throat above an open-collared beige shirt was more than a little disturbing.

"I'm beginning to like this city," Kennedy said, and Hayley wondered if she was just imagining the ripple of laughter beneath his words.

She shuddered to think she was so transparent.

After several moments of silence, Hayley slanted him a covert look, catching him in an unguarded moment as he looked over the wine list. The angles of his cheekbones were harsh, his nose straight, his jaw determined—maybe even a little arrogant. It was a face that reflected a man used to authority, a dynamic man, one most would be unwilling to cross.

Having always prided herself on being a woman attracted to sensitive, unassuming, *un-macho* males, she wondered what in the world she was doing here with him. Yet, just because Kennedy was dynamic didn't mean he wasn't sensitive; he'd already proven he was. Moreover, he possessed a lot of other traits she admired: forthrightness, honesty, intelligence, creativity, virility. . . .

Her mouth curved wryly. Well, he certainly had it, didn't he? And there was no point in denying that she was susceptible to it.

Feeling his eyes on her, and ridiculously afraid that he might read her thoughts, Hayley tried to keep with their earlier conversation. "Portland's a lot smaller than Los Angeles," she observed.

Kennedy smiled. "And a lot prettier."

Hayley's breath caught. His silver-green eyes chased hers. The moment between them spun out, the edges of the room receding, noises dimming. She blinked rapidly, her lips parting to say—*something*. . . .

With a huge effort, she dragged her gaze from his compelling face. She cleared her throat, and said lightly, reaching for her menu, "You're just trying to turn my head."

"I'm trying to get your attention. All of it." His hand closed over hers. She froze instantly.

Kennedy plucked the menu from her nerveless fingers, setting it aside. "Tell me if that's possible, or if I'm just wasting my time."

He was dazzling her with the full force of his personality. Hayley's resistance was melting; she could practically feel it physically slipping away.

Her lashes flickered. The time for game playing was over. "It's entirely too possible, I'm afraid."

"Ah . . ." Kennedy rubbed his nose thoughtfully. "Key words, those." At her look, he said meaningfully, "'I'm afraid.'"

Hayley drew a long breath, lifting her chin. "Okay. Maybe I *am* afraid."

Kennedy leaned forward. They were finally getting somewhere. "Of me?"

"Of involvement. Involvement—with you," she amended. "I have a right to be."

He sensed she was trying to tell him something important. "What are we talking about now—my being the defendant and you the prosecuting attorney?"

"No. I—"

The waiter's untimely intervention cut Hayley off. Kennedy frowned, impatient to learn every fascinating detail about this woman who interested him so much. Telling himself to bide his time, he selected a bottle of wine from one of the local vineyards, and they both ordered. After the wine had been delivered, uncorked and given to Kennedy for tasting, and the waiter had discreetly disappeared, he continued his gentle prodding.

"Then you must have been talking about your ex-husband," he said, pouring her a glass of sparkling rosé.

Hayley hadn't mentally put it into those terms—she'd been thinking solely about Kennedy. She started to protest, then stopped herself. In truth, yes, Gerald, and her dismal relationship with him, was probably the very root of her reluctance. Who Kennedy was, as opposed to who she was, was just added difficulty.

Hayley sipped her wine, considering. "I told you I had a miserable marriage, and that I wasn't looking for another relationship. That still stands."

"But . . . ?"

She shook the tumbled curtain of her hair, a gesture which revealed her indecision more eloquently than words. Her eyes were a clear, but troubled gray, as she said softly, "Maybe I should ask you what you want."

Kennedy wasn't nearly so undecided; he'd been hooked from the first time he'd set eyes on her. Mouth curving in unconscious sensuality, he warned, "You might not like the answer."

"Try me."

He turned her palm over, rubbing it with his

thumb, his eyes locked to hers. Hayley's heartbeat quickened at the hunger that flashed from his eyes in glints of silver.

He emphasized each word with critical distinctness. "I—want—you."

Hayley instinctively pulled back, but his hand trapped hers. Locked as she was to him, inside she was fleeing, running at breakneck speed away from him, from all he represented.

"Hadn't you guessed?" he said with a soft smile.

Hayley's face whitened with wild panic before years of training hid it beneath her professional facade. Of course she'd guessed; she felt the same. But putting it into words was so difficult.

Her lips quivered into a smile. "The trouble is, there are no guarantees."

"No. There are no guarantees."

It was like agreeing to disagree. The problem existed, and there was no way around it, and talking about it didn't make any difference. Was she really crazy enough to jump into a situation, eyes open, that had no security, just because a man wanted her?

"I can't make promises that would be impossible to keep." Kennedy filled the sudden gap of silence. "I wouldn't. What we have might not be enough for you in itself, might not be what you *need*. But if it means anything to you, you're proof to me that I'm capable of falling in love again."

Hayley's throat hurt. Her eyes were naked with disbelief. What was he saying to her? My God, the vulnerability in his face showed how much that honesty cost him. He'd laid himself bare, and she knew it was something he rarely—if ever—did; his face said it all.

"Why?" she whispered incredulously. This kind of intensity was perilous. She had absolutely no defense.

He laughed a trifle shakily. "I don't know if there's an answer to that. I didn't think I could ever really feel so drawn, so compelled to someone else."

Hayley was carved in stone. She didn't believe this was happening; yet she knew intimately what he meant. But did he really feel the same, or was he just that aware of what she wanted—needed—to hear?

Kennedy's lashes lowered, his gaze drifting toward her opened palm. Hayley had the insane urge to ball her hand into a fist, as if somehow that could protect her.

A moment of tense introspection followed, when the lines of disillusionment bracketing Kennedy's mouth tightened. "I had a terrible marriage too," he said at length.

Hayley's eyes were like his, focused on their touching hands. She heard restraint, even aversion, in his tone. What he was about to say wasn't easy for him.

"My wife was beautiful and volatile, and the most ambitious human being I've ever met," he said flatly. "We lasted three years and then she left me for a studio executive who is now head of his own production company. She's the co-owner, and, knowing my ex—" Kennedy's smile was more ironic than bitter "—she's running that company by herself."

Hayley knew this wasn't a story many were privy to. While eaten up with curiosity, she half-feared growing this close to him. They were crossing those nebulous

bonds of friendship and hurtling straight for something a thousand times more dangerous. But she
didn't protest. She waited.

"Anyway." His breath came out on a sigh. "To
make a long story short, I was very negative on
relationships after that. I had an extremely narrow
viewpoint: All women were treacherous, scheming
and, therefore, an unnecessary evil. Being sued by
that actress was just icing on the cake." His eyes swept
to Hayley's, gauging her reaction so far. After a
moment, he added, "It didn't help that she'd tried to
further her career with me by inviting herself to my
casting couch first."

"Oh, my God." This brutal slice of Hollywood life
was more than Hayley had bargained for. It was pure
insanity.

"Not everyone, of course, is like that," Kennedy
assured her quickly. "I've met hundreds of honest,
hardworking women in the film industry. It was just a
case of one thing following too closely on another,
and suddenly, I didn't want a woman near me."
Innate sensuality curved his mouth once more. "A
very stupid and basically frustrating decision."

Hayley's eyes fastened on a drop of condensation
on her wineglass. She counted to ten, very slowly.
"And now . . . ?"

"And now I think it's time for a new philosophy."
Kennedy's hand curled hers inside the shelter of his.
"You know I'm attracted to you. You have to know
how I feel about you."

Yes, she knew. He wanted her, as a man wants a
woman. A very simple, straightforward kind of thing.

But was it really?

She looked down at the rich folds of her rose silk dress—the dress she'd chosen for him—and wondered. She knew without a doubt he was asking for an affair, and after that, let the chips fall where they may. Unfortunately, it wasn't what she wanted, but then, what *did* she want? Marriage? That was too farfetched even to consider! To be left to the lifestyle she'd grown accustomed to? Alone, but not necessarily lonely?

"I know," she said, swallowing hard, "that this is putting the cart before the horse, but I have to ask."

"Go ahead."

Hayley glanced out the window, then back to the intimate coupling of their hands, then to his face. "I'm not into . . . short-term . . . relationships. I haven't—" Hayley licked her lips, her cheeks flushing in abashment. She was ridiculously tongue-tied.

"You haven't slept with anyone since your husband," Kennedy put it gently.

This was painful for her. More than she'd ever anticipated it would be. "It's more than that," she said in utter sincerity. "I haven't had an emotional relationship since before I wedded my husband."

Her marriage had been the emptiest, loneliest experience she'd ever gone through. Gerald was simply never there. She believed, to this day, that he'd never intentionally meant to hurt her, but he was uncaring, selfish and totally baffled by her chronic unhappiness. Any feelings she'd had for him were deadened the first time he'd admitted to seeing another woman. But it was his unshakable, bizarre belief that she shouldn't even care that had killed her feelings entirely. She was wasting emotion on a person who'd never fully grown up. Gerald was an everlasting child.

"So the question is," Hayley forged on, "what happens in the end? Do we just go our separate ways and say, 'Thanks, nice knowing you'?" Her gray eyes were luminous with remembered sadness. "Emotionally, Kennedy, I don't know if I could do that. And I'm too realistic to fantasize about a relationship that has no end. Everything ends."

"He really did a number on you, didn't he?"

Kennedy felt an unreasonable fury at the man who'd been Hayley's husband. And that fury was magnified when she instantly tried to defend the man.

"I'm not looking for sympathy. Gerald was Gerald, period. He wasn't made for me, that's all."

Kennedy's mouth twisted. "Whatever he did, love, it was enough to convince you that no other man is made for you either."

"That's not true." Hayley shook her head, urgently trying to make him understand. "I'm just more cautious now."

"You're downright scared, sweetheart."

The fine line of her dark honey brows drew together in silent protest. When Kennedy's palms suddenly held her face she pulled back, gray eyes flying open in shock.

"That's fear, love," he said solemnly.

He was unnerving her, something that rarely ever happened. And she didn't like the feeling one bit. "I'm not good at pretending, Kennedy." He refused to let go of her. Her face was a captive, held only inches from his determined one. "There's a better than good chance that one of us, if not both, will lose from this relationship."

"I'm willing to chance it."

Life's inequities hit her like a blow. "Of course you are!" she accused, seeing the future roll out before her. "You're a man. You have less to lose."

His hands tightened and she heard his sharp intake of breath. "Well, now there's an interesting case of discrimination!" His eyes darkened with anger and drilled into hers. The corners of his mouth drew down. "Who says, just because you're female, that you're more susceptible to pain? You think I couldn't be hurt?"

It was a rhetorical question. Hayley could only stare mutely.

His hands dropped and he pulled back, his shoulders slumping. "You don't give yourself enough credit, lady. I've got a feeling you could rip me apart."

Hayley's breath trembled in her throat. Kennedy's knack for leaving her shaken, vulnerable, was unerring. He wasn't Gerald, that was for certain. But then she'd never thought he was.

But aren't you subconsciously accusing him of Gerald's worst transgressions? Isn't that why you're fighting him? Isn't it?

Her hand touched her throat. "I'm sorry," she said helplessly.

"You weren't being exactly fair," he said quietly, and Hayley inwardly cringed, knowing he was right. Hadn't she just witnessed Matthew's pain over

Sheryl? Just because she'd been hurt before didn't mean she had cornered the market on pain. . . .

She bowed her head to avoid his gaze and Kennedy found himself looking at the satiny crown of her head. "There's always an element of risk in everything," he said gently. "Otherwise life would be pretty dull."

Hayley sipped from her wineglass, aware that she'd barely touched her meal. "I'm very partial to dull."

She looked up at his sudden stillness, and found herself drowning in the sensual silvery green depths of his eyes. "Somehow," he said deliberately, pulling down every fence she'd erected in the space of a single instant, "I don't think that's true."

Hayley chewed her food without tasting it, offering no comment. The wine was blurring the edges of her mind. She couldn't fight him anymore; she was beginning to lose sight of any reason to.

Kennedy was absorbed in the delicate pinkness of her mouth as she ate. He hadn't meant to be so open; his privacy was painfully important to him. But it had been the only way to touch her—so he had gambled. . . .

And he suspected that he'd won.

Kennedy stretched his long legs, trying to ignore the partially pleasant, partially agonizing, first stirrings of arousal. It mystified him, the effect this woman had on him, but he'd never been a man to turn his back on a puzzle—especially one as intriguing as Hayley Sinclair.

He was surprised, however, when after her long introspection, Hayley dared to ask, "What did you mean about falling in love?"

Her honesty was one of the things he liked best about her. "Anything's possible," he said, admiring the softened planes of her face. "Though, I have to admit, I've been a bit of a skeptic for a long time."

"You've never been in love?"

Kennedy could feel her curiosity but wasn't put off by it. He leaned forward on his elbows. "Have you?" he countered.

Hayley tried to field the question nonchalantly. "Not lately." She turned away involuntarily, unequipped to deal with the blatant appreciation of his gaze. "At least not in this lifetime."

The muted lights of the restaurant made the streaks of gold in her hair softly glisten. She was unbelievably, maddeningly touchable, yet Kennedy knew she was still out of reach. She kept herself that way, tantalizing and distant, and totally captivating.

"Then we're two of a kind," he answered, touching the rim of his glass against hers with a musical ping.

Hayley half smiled, flirting with danger. "But anything's possible, right?"

His rich laughter rolled from his chest, a response to her unexpected spontaneity. Heads turned, but neither Hayley nor Kennedy noticed.

"That's right. And I'm ready for the possible to become the probable. Let's leave."

As he scraped back his chair, Hayley had no choice but to go with him. If she didn't object, she knew things would progress just as Kennedy hoped they would.

And what about you? she asked herself. *What do you want?*

An impossible question to answer.

Hayley shivered in the cold evening air, her mouth parting in surprise as Kennedy dropped his arm familiarly over shoulders. His finger shushed her lips.

"Don't say a word. I've had more than enough talking for one evening."

She complied with a nervous smile, and they stood quietly together outside the rustic stone building. A steep wooden staircase from the top of the cliff to the riverbank provided access to the catwalk that linked the houseboats with the piers. Of one mind, they walked to the top of the stairs, gazing down at the soft glow from the string of lights that dipped between the houseboats.

"Want to walk down?" Hayley glanced at his shadowed face.

"Not especially." He turned her slowly in his arms, his breath warm against her forehead. "But I'm willing to make sacrifices." She felt the featherlight touch of a kiss on her lips, then he captured her hand and led her down the stairs.

There was no wind, and the rain had stopped several hours earlier. The steps were still damp, however, and they proceeded cautiously, moving down the angled flights with extreme care. Hayley nearly lost her footing twice, but both times Kennedy's strong, guiding hand kept her upright.

"This might not have been such a great idea," she admitted, her breath smoking in the frigid air.

"Hmmm. I've got better ones."

Kennedy stopped on the last step, giving Hayley no

warning as her body crashed into his. Her arms went wide, but he caught her easily, swooping her close. The intimacy was so unexpected that Hayley couldn't move. Her breasts were trapped against his powerful chest, her legs slipping beneath her, the smooth planes of her sliding downward in his arms, across his stomach, his waist, then the hard definition of his hips and thighs.

She was breathless and now aware of something else. His desire strained urgently against her; she couldn't ignore it. She righted herself on shaking legs.

"Kennedy . . ."

Desire gleamed from his half-closed eyes. He groped hungrily for her mouth, warm and sweet and still partially open. A low groan escaped him, the plea of a starving man.

Hayley was bombarded with sensation—the desperate urgency of his tongue, his deepening desire, the convulsive movement of his hands against the small of her back. She leaned her head back, giving a long, soulful sigh in answer to the question he hadn't asked.

"I want you. . . ." His thickened murmur only further enflamed her. "I want you, Hayley."

And I want you . . .

"Oh, love, love . . ." He buried his face in the richness of her hair. It billowed around him like a wild, beautiful wind.

She understood that he was trying to bring himself under control, that he hadn't intended this sudden assault, that he felt he was rushing her. Her love for him overflowed.

She kissed his nape, the firm line of his jaw, the sweetly roughened curve of his cheek. He accepted her caresses in utter stillness, his hands gripping her shoulders, as if he were afraid that to move would break the spell.

It was a sign that things were changing; she was changing. And beginning to accept the powerful forces that bound them together.

She let her arms slide down his, until they were two arm's lengths apart, their fingertips barely touching. "So . . . what do you think?" she asked, turning, her burnished gold hair sweeping around her.

"Beautiful." His eyes followed her mobile face, not the panorama of water, timber and inky night surrounding them.

"You're deliberately misunderstanding me."

"Oh." Kennedy let go of her long enough to rub his chin with one hand, pondering her question as if it were very serious indeed. He turned up the collar on his coat. "Colder than what I'm used to," he admitted.

"But tremendous?"

Forest-black firs lined the shore opposite. Only an occasional blur from a light broke the air of remoteness, and sounds of the city were indistinct murmurs in a quiet night. Not even the noise from the Inn above could be heard.

"Tremendous," Kennedy agreed, the hoarseness of his tone sending a shiver skating down Hayley's spine.

With a feeling of incredulity, Hayley said softly, "I haven't thought about the trial once this evening."

His thumb slipped under the curtain of her hair, moving with tiny circular motions against her nape. "Neither have I. And even if I had, it would only be because the trial was the fate that brought us together." His hand crept to the front of her throat, one finger dipping to the lowest scoop of her neckline. "You're not the prosecuting attorney anymore, Hayley. And I'm not the defendant. Those two people are gone and you and I are all that's left."

"That's too simple," she breathed, her attention fastened on the tip of his finger.

"No, it's not. You're the one making things complex."

She swallowed. His finger was moving in delicate semicircles. "I don't mean to."

"Mmmm."

Hayley could feel her nipples responding. They were suddenly rigid against the sheerness of her bra, poking outward, visible beneath the dark silk of her dress. "What does that mean?" she asked breathlessly.

"Highly sophisticated defense mechanisms," he muttered. His finger painted a lazy circle around her nipple, an audacious move that left Hayley completely breathless.

"Kennedy . . ."

"What?"

Before she could prevent him, he began slowly moving downward, kissing her forehead lightly, then her cheeks, her chin, the arch of her neck. Downward and downward, further, and further, until all she could see was his dark head dipped against her breast. But she could still *feel!* And the feeling was hot, and electric, and melting as his mouth unexpectedly closed over the nipple his finger had brought to budding life.

Hayley's eyes widened in surprise. She moaned in protest. "Oh, no, no . . . what are you doing to me?"

His hand had found the curve of her hips, fingers growing bold with desire. Hayley was drawn tight as a bow, her body quivering. Instinctively her hands wound into his hair, thick, vital, strands crushed beneath the agony of her indecision.

"Trust me, sweetheart," Kennedy murmured. "Just—let me . . ."

This was what she feared. This was what she wanted! Every nerve was on fire, and she was powerless to stop the already turning tide of total passion.

Her hands now trembled on the broad width of his shoulders but inside she was clawing him closer, begging him to assuage the ache he'd created within her.

"Oh, Kennedy, I don't know." The fabric was wet and cool against her breast when his mouth lifted, hot and silky when it returned.

He was murmuring to her. "Hayley . . . love . . . beautiful, love . . ."

It was the speed of it that was so dizzying. His tongue was flicking at her nipple. She felt his hands move down her legs, to the hem of her dress, sliding it upward with an unhurried determination. A bell rang in Hayley's mind. Things were totally out of control!

Her hands dug into the flesh of his shoulders,

urgent and fearful. He was crossing boundaries she couldn't yet allow!

"Kennedy!"

"Shh . . ."

His thumb had found the much too sensitive curve of her inner thigh. In a moment she would be completely lost. Begging him to stop in the only way she could, Hayley grabbed his face between her palms, guiding his ravaging mouth to the trembling expectation of hers.

The eagerness with which she pressed herself against him was a mixed signal, part relief at forestalling his intimate attack, but part honest desire too. With urgent shifts of her body, Hayley moved to accommodate his masculine angles in a totally uninhibited way.

It was the final fissure in the dam of Kennedy's control. His arms closed possessively over her, his hard contours fitted tightly to her yielding ones. Hayley's soft moan of final protest was lost beneath the conquest of his mouth.

Kennedy's breath was ragged. Hayley's sounded in rapid counterpoint to his. His hips moved with a restrained urgency that shattered Hayley's equilibrium. She could only cling to him.

A shudder passed through his taut muscles. "Oh, Hayley . . . I can't take much more of this," he groaned.

She shook her head, burying her face in the sanctuary of his shoulder.

Kennedy's heart was thudding heavily. "What does

that mean?" he asked, his patience exquisite. She could feel the stretched-wire tension of his muscles.

"Yes." She could hear the huskiness of her own voice. "It means yes."

He extricated himself from her arms slowly, tilting up her chin to see the paleness of her face. In a voice that was ragged and hungry, he muttered, "I want to make love to you. Tonight. I don't want to wait."

Hayley's eyes were eloquent. Waiting was out of the question for either one of them.

Kennedy let out a long breath, his face clearing as he led her to the stairs. Later, she didn't remember the climb; the ride to her apartment was also vague. She could recall the companionship, and the tense undercurrent of sensual desire, but the actual words escaped her. Her mind had been spinning ahead; Kennedy's had been too.

The rain returned with a vengeance as Kennedy parked his car on the street below Hayley's apartment. They ran as fast as they could up the dark steps to her door, both out of breath when they reached the shelter of the eave; Hayley noticeably more so.

"You must keep yourself in good shape," she observed, panting.

"Mmm-hmm." He drew a long breath, admiring her backside as she leaned over the lock. "You can't live in Southern California without a great body and a tan."

Hayley turned the key and made a face at the laughter lurking behind his eyes. "I probably deserved that."

"Damn right you did. You're a snob, Hayley Sinclair."

Kennedy shut the door behind him and watched as Hayley took off her coat, her face changing with mock affront.

"A snob? How can you say that?" She placed one firm fist on her hip, intending to say a lot more, when the intimacy of their situation—the *reason* they'd come to her apartment—suddenly hit home.

"Because you are," Kennedy replied, his mouth twisting amusedly. He saw the animation fade from her face and ached to take her in his arms. He wanted to assure her that her fears were groundless, that he would never hurt her.

His long strides ate up the distance between them before she could move. "Actually, you're an anti-snob," he said, hands on her shoulders, thumbs meeting at the shadowed hollow of her throat.

"Anti-snob?" Kennedy's thumb stroked her throat, his touch downy soft. She felt it hover over her pulsebeat. She was unable to think, waiting for him to touch her again.

"The last thing you want to do is be in the company of someone rich, or famous," he said quietly. "Especially us Hollywood types. I think it spoils your image of yourself."

Hayley swallowed. "What image is that?"

He was watching his thumb with a concentration that made Hayley feel weak. "Oh," he said distractedly, "Defender of the people. Robin Hood reincarnated in Maid Marian's body."

"I told you before, I'm not that selfless. I have to eat, too."

"But you're not greedy, either, sweetheart." His head dipped, his lips brushing hers.

"You could be wrong about me, y'know." The brief feel of his mouth was stirring all those responses. She couldn't quite prevent herself from licking her lips, and she could feel his burning gaze center on her mouth. "I might be in this business solely for the money. If Claudia Jeffries had gotten her million-dollar settlement, I certainly would have prospered too."

Kennedy's body stiffened almost imperceptibly, as if she'd suddenly reminded him of something he'd nearly forgotten. It jarred Hayley, but a heartbeat later his mouth touched hers again, this time pulling her bottom lip between the warmth of his. "But that's not why you tried her case, is it, love?"

"Isn't it?"

He shook his head slowly from side to side. "You wanted to set a precedent, remember? You have very noble intentions."

Dimly, she felt there was something to beware here. Something he'd said that had awakened sleeping doubts. But for the life of her she couldn't remember what it was, and Kennedy's deep voice, sweet breath and persuasive touch were making it hard even to concentrate on their conversation.

"What are your other clients like?" he asked. "I'd venture to guess very few are like Claudia Jeffries."

Hayley thought about Tom Wilson. Something of a chauvinist, perhaps, but she had to admit that Kennedy had a point—she did feel he was getting a raw deal. That was why she wanted to represent him.

But for some reason she had to argue with Kennedy. She sensed it was important, though why she should have to defend her capitalism escaped her. "I still don't work for free."

His tongue was working magic on her. "You're just talking to stall me," he murmured.

Hayley was affronted. "That's not true. I—"

His impatient movement cut her off. "Then," he demanded, "tell me how you feel about this: 'Blessed are the meek, for they shall pave the way for the ruthless.'"

"That's terrible!"

He laughed at her shocked sensibilities. "I rest my case, counselor," he drawled. "Now shut that beautiful mouth and come here. . . ."

Here was in the possessive circle of his arms. Hayley closed her eyes to smoky gray glints. "You're a hard man to say no to, Mr. Taft," she murmured.

"Then don't. All I want to hear from you is yes."

But she didn't have time to say anything. His mouth captured hers with utter possessiveness, hard and demanding and silently warning her that the time for feeble excuses had passed. She sensed she could still say no, but this final gambit was his last.

Trust me, sweetheart.

She wanted to with a passion that scared her. What if she were to make a mistake . . . *again?*

There's an element of risk in everything.

Her mouth opened beneath the persuasion of his, and immediately his lips gentled. He took time to savor each change of texture, from the smoothness of her teeth, to the warm invitation of her tongue, enjoying each moment of increasing intimacy.

Her hands slid down the lapels of his jacket, knowing an urge to strip it from his back. He read her thoughts, removing it with deft movements, only breaking contact with her mouth for the briefest of moments.

Then she could feel his heat through his shirt, and her hands encountered the hard muscles of his torso. Hayley's heart was running away from her and she was trembling.

He smoothed back her hair, releasing a carefully controlled breath. "Don't be afraid," he murmured.

"I'm not. Not the way you mean."

He kissed her temple, his jaw gently rubbing the curve of her cheekbone. "How do I mean?"

"I'm not afraid of loving you."

Her painful sincerity caused him to look at her closely. "Then you're afraid of the morning after. Don't be."

She gave him a shadowy smile. "I'm afraid of letting you down," she admitted.

"Oh, love." His laugh was short, almost harsh. "You couldn't. Things are way, way past that point."

A warm sensation flooded Hayley. She'd never had a man admit to wanting her that much. Gerald had always been lukewarm in their lovemaking, even with as little of it as there was, and though rationally knowing it wasn't all her fault, Hayley had always harbored deep-seeded doubts about her desirability. Now her feminine ego soared.

She let her lashes flutter closed as his lips found the sensitive edges of her ear, nibbling delicately. "You're good for me," she whispered.

Kennedy's silent laughter was full of delight. "So I've been telling you . . ."

He was pleased that she'd finally crossed that toughest boundary. She was beginning to trust him.

His fingers found the tab to her zipper and she felt it whisper downward. A tremor ran under her skin at the first feel of his palm against her flesh. Kennedy immediately cuddled her near, drawing her closer to his male heat.

Outside the rain poured in an unbroken symphony. Kennedy guided her slowly toward her bedroom, and Hayley felt that strange lethargic feeling of inevitability descend once more.

He didn't press the switch, but the beam from one of the outdoor floodlights sent soft, rain-blurred illumination into the room. Hayley waited in the darkness, feeling his fingers slide her dress from her shoulders.

His mouth touched the curve of her shoulder, beginning a slow discovery that found its way to the fluttering pulse at her neck. With a deft flick, her bra was unclasped. It followed the path of her dress, until she stood nearly naked before him.

She was breathing so rapidly her breasts trembled, milky curves beckoning in the uncertain light. At the sight of her, Kennedy groaned low in his throat.

"You're so beautiful," he whispered, then his palm shaped the curve of her breast, and his mouth encircled her nipple.

Hayley's legs went weak. Her hand found the back of his rain-dampened hair and pulled him closer as her head lolled back in ecstacy. She felt him completely undress her, then the sudden tipping of her world as he lifted her malleable form to the bed.

She lifted her arms to him, bereft for the few moments it took him to unbutton his shirt. His eyes were on her, and after yanking the last button free, he lay down beside her in urgent impatience.

Her hands roamed over the startlingly taut muscles of his back, and Hayley moaned weakly at the exquisitely slow way he was arousing her.

"I want you," he whispered hoarsely, somewhere near the sensitive lobe of her ear. "But it's not just want. I've never felt this way about a woman before."

It was exactly what she wanted to hear. She shifted restlessly, feeling his hard contours, the leashed control that said it was costing him to wait, but that he cared enough to take his time with her.

She slid a hand down his chest, touching his male nipple. The tremor that ran beneath his skin made her bold, and she followed her explorations with her mouth. His hands were clenched in her hair.

"Hayley . . . ," he groaned, his body burning with the need for her.

It was a beautiful power, knowing what she could do to him, a sweet torture that made Hayley as breathless as he. She moaned involuntarily, an answer to the rasped sound of his labored breathing.

When her hands encountered the buckle of his belt, she quickly undid it. But she fumbled over the zipper, and after several exquisitely painful moments, Kennedy swept her hands aside and removed the rest of his clothes with a few supple twists of his body.

"God," he breathed, lying beside her, his hipbone hard against her thigh. He threw one leg over her, entrapping her, and his hand ran over the satin flatness of her abdomen.

The delicacy of his touch made her burn for more. She quivered beneath his hands, her back arching, silently begging. He answered with a kiss that consumed her mouth, and she shifted her legs beneath his, urging a more intimate touch.

He deliberately delayed, his hands and mouth discovering all the delights of her nakedness, from the shell pinkness of her earlobe to the hill of her abdomen; from her soft, trembling lips to the mounded fullness of her breast; from the arch of her throat to the warm, darkness of her inner thigh.

Hayley's insides were screaming with need. She tried to tell him in soft moans and whispered sounds, in the driving gyrations of her hips. When his sensual torture continued, she placed her hands firmly on his buttocks, intent upon ending her torment.

She sensed, rather than felt, the satisfied smile that curved his mouth, and was appalled. He was doing it on purpose! But then she became aware of his strong, potent maleness, and with a half smile stealing across her swollen lips, Hayley began an exploration of her own.

Her fingers traveled slowly down his thigh, exploring the corded muscles, feeling the heat beneath the hair-roughened surface. She moved languidly, fighting the growing needs of her body, and was rewarded with a quickening to his breath that was almost a rasp.

"Hayley . . . ," he warned, but it only fired her desire to arouse him.

She swept a fingertip along his inner thigh and moved her hips tightly against his, feeling the hard shudder that passed through him. She was so intent upon this endeavor that she missed his silent tightening of muscle, the sharp intake of his breath.

Suddenly she was pinned beneath him, his hips angled over hers, her buttocks cupped in the steel grip of his hands. He moved once, the intimate contact sending heat racing through every nerve.

"You make it—impossible—to wait," he said, his jaw clenching.

A fine mist of sweat covered her body. Hayley stared into his eyes, hammered silver in the dim light. "Then don't . . ."

"Oh, love," he groaned, as, with one vital thrust of his body, they became one.

She felt the great need in him, the fierce shuddering that ran through him, the ravaging desire that fought with his iron will. There was no need for him to wait. All Hayley's nerves were at a fever's pitch. She spread her palms upon the tight sinews of his hips and moved with beautiful, rhythmic need.

Kennedy was at her mercy. The world exploded around him, pleasure expanding with each movement. He felt the imminent moment of release, felt Hayley's increased tension, heard the building sounds of her pleasure.

She was unaware of anything but the moment of shuddering ecstacy until she felt Kennedy's answering fulfillment. It was a glorious, rushing, expanding fire that seemed to shake the heavens, and she was spent and gasping when it was over.

After several moments of lassitude, he levered his weight away, to lie beside her, cradling her in the warm comfort of his arms. "Beautiful, beautiful Hayley," he murmured, his heartbeat still strong and rapid. "And you worried you would let me down."

Hayley buried her face in his shoulder, hiding a smile. "I take it I didn't."

He laughed softly. "You lovely little tease. My God . . ." He inhaled a long breath and blew it out slowly. "This is too good to be true."

Hayley cocked her head, opening one languid eye. "My feelings exactly. But I'm willing to run with it as long as it lasts."

Kennedy's head turned on the pillow. "What makes you so certain it won't?"

"Last? I gave you all those arguments earlier."

His finger meditatively traced the curve of her chin. "That was before," he said lazily. "You won't be able to convince me so easily now."

She didn't believe him. Things passed. There was no stopping the march of time. But she did appreciate knowing that, for the moment, she held him captive, woman to man, lover to lover.

"I won't even try to," she said, stretching with satisfaction.

"Good. Because I'm staying the night."

The warmth and security of his arms lulled Hayley

to sleep. She refused to think about tomorrow. "I wouldn't have it any other way," she murmured, stifling a yawn.

He gently kissed her forehead. "I wouldn't let you, love."

And for Kennedy, the words had extra meaning. If he wasn't falling in love with Hayley, it was something just as meaningful. And he had no intention of letting her go. Today, tomorrow or maybe ever . . .

Chapter Six

"Leave it down."

Hayley's hand stopped in mid-twist, her chignon falling into scattered tresses. In her dresser mirror she met Kennedy's lazy stare, the sight of snowy white sheets surrounding his lean, dark chest making her pulse involuntarily accelerate.

"I can't wear it like this to work," she objected. "I'm the lady lawyer, remember?"

"Hayley Sinclair, Attorney-at-Law. I remember." A sardonic smile flashed across his face. "I guarantee you a better success rate with the jurors—at least the male jurors—if you leave it down."

"Wrong." Hayley resumed work on her hair. "Jurors expect a highly professional appearance. Besides, your theory won't be put to the test anyway because I'm not due in court today."

She purposely ignored his unconscious male beauty, the shape of limb and muscle she could see above the sheet, the hidden parts she could vividly imagine. Waking up with him had held no embarrassment for her, but she'd been horrified at the late hour. For the last ten minutes she'd been rushing around like a mad woman, cursing the druglike sleep that had made her miss her morning shower.

She tried not to remember that it was the security of Kennedy's warm body curled next to hers that had given her that beautiful, dreamless sleep. She couldn't afford to get too used to him.

"Then don't go to work today."

She dared another glance at him. His arms were behind his head, his eyes half-closed, the humor bracketing his mouth a silent challenge. There was nothing Hayley would have liked better than to spend the day with him—after all, it could be her last. . . .

"Easy for you to say," Hayley responded lightly. "You're not the one with a job beckoning."

"Not today, at any rate."

Hayley turned away, pushing diamond studs through her pierced ears. She didn't want to think about his job, about the fact that he would soon be leaving for California. Her lips twisted ruefully. The morning after had come—and it was filled with fears and doubts.

"Hayley . . ."

"What?"

She frowned at the press of her champagne-colored jacket, pretending total absorption in the lay of her lapels. Her hands nervously retied the loose bow of her mauve blouse.

"I don't have much time left. Come here." He patted the spot beside him, where she'd slept.

His words made it all seem more horribly real. "I know you don't have much time left," she said quickly. She couldn't address the problem now. She couldn't face it! She didn't have the skills to appear nonchalant.

He sat up, tension tightening his jaw. "You want me to come there?" he asked pointedly.

A vision passed her inner eye: sinewy muscle, tan legs, dark skin melting into whiter areas that rarely saw the sun. . . . "No." Hayley quickly crossed the room on noiseless stockinged feet. She didn't want her equilibrium assaulted by his utter maleness now.

But when she perched herself on the bed's edge, his arm swooped out and tugged her to the disturbing warmth of his bare chest. "Don't shut me out," he said tensely. "I haven't left yet. I want you, Hayley. *You.* And a state line isn't going to keep me away from you."

Her palm had centered over his steady heartbeat. She desperately wanted to believe him, and it was that desperation that she feared more than anything. She wanted him so much—too much. It could only be trouble, and pain, in the future.

"How—how long do you intend to stay in Portland?"

"I don't know. As long as I can." He tried to smooth the little lines that creased her forehead, hating himself for being the cause, unable to offer more than half promises. "I'll be here tonight when you get home."

Hayley swallowed, absurdly upset. "You tempt me to believe the impossible, Kennedy."

She couldn't read the sound he made. Was it exasperation? Impatience? Defeat?

But the kiss he placed on her lips melted any doubts she had that he might be just placating her. The hunger was still there, undisguised and burning.

"Then believe it, love. Remember, we're making the impossible, possible, and the possible, probable."

"Your words," she reminded him.

His silver-green eyes bore into hers. "You have to meet me halfway."

"Oh, Kennedy." She pulled her face from the touch and persuasion of his, hurting. With painful honesty, she whispered, "You know I'd do anything to keep you with me."

"Do I?"

She glanced back. He wasn't searching for compliments. The grimness around his mouth, the anxiety of waiting for her response, said he really needed to know.

It gave her courage. She touched her fingertip to his bottom lip, and said softly, "Yes, you do."

His hand slipped beneath her jacket, curving possessively beneath one breast. Hayley's pulse responded instantly, and for a moment she let herself respond to his lazy seduction. His mouth captured hers, his tongue beginning a slow exploration she was beginning to know. The palm she'd placed against his chest remained firm, however; a reminder that she still had to go to work.

"Mmmm. Don't discourage me, love. We've got lots of time."

Hayley's drowsy senses awoke with a jolt. Lots of time was exactly what they didn't have. She tried to extricate herself from his embrace but his arms tightened.

"Kennedy . . ."

"I won't let you get away," he murmured.

"You don't have a choice."

"Don't I?" His brows lifted in challenge.

"*I* don't have a choice."

"Make love to me one more time and I'll let you go."

"I don't have time!"

"I'll be quick."

His erotic suggestions were driving her to distraction. She wriggled madly to escape, causing him to emit a deep groan of satisfaction that she was sure was largely faked.

"You're impossible," she declared breathlessly, pushing against the wall of his chest in earnest.

She could feel the uneven weight of her hair the instant after Kennedy jerked out the pins. She glared at him in total frustration. "Now look what you've done."

"I see," he drawled sexily.

She scowled at him, but it was hard to be truly angry when he was just voicing her own longings. "You're going to make me late."

"Call in sick."

The mauve silk bow was slowly being untied. Kennedy wrapped it carefully around his index finger, winding his hand closer and closer to her throat.

Hayley was losing sight of her objections, was amazed that she could be so un-*herself!* "I couldn't lie to my own father," she breathed.

"It wouldn't be a lie. You're lovesick. We both are."

He buried his face into the open throat of her blouse, his tongue touching the throb of her pulse. Hayley felt the invading weakness, the wild, beautiful desire that only Kennedy could create.

I'm falling in love with you.

Hayley knew it was true. But she wasn't just falling—she *was* in love with him.

He pulled her beneath the weight of his naked body, unmindful of the destruction to her clothes. Hayley didn't mind either. All she could concentrate on were his shaking fingers as he undid the tiny, pearl-shaped buttons that ran down the front of her blouse. . . .

Hayley's cheeks were tinged the bright pink of embarrassment, her poise as windblown as the swirling strands of hair that had escaped her chignon, as she hurried into her office and snatched up the imperatively buzzing telephone.

"Hello?" Her pleated skirt—blue this time, after she'd had to change suits—revealed a shapely knee as she leaned against the edge of her desk.

"Hayley?" Jason Sinclair's voice was full of puzzlement. "Where have you been?"

Closing her eyes on a silent groan, Hayley enumerated all the reasons she should have left Kennedy Taft alone. She was never late to work.

"Sorry, I'm running late this morning. I just walked in the door." Slipping her raincoat from her shoulders, she felt her omission about Kennedy settling over her with the heavy guilt of an out-and-out lie. "Did I miss something important?" she asked anxiously. "There was nothing on my calendar."

"No, no." He dismissed her tardiness without a second thought. "It's Warren Smythe. He wants to see you this afternoon. He's planning to file an appeal as soon as possible, and needs your help."

His dry tone didn't even register with Hayley. Her heart had plummeted to her stomach. Warren Smythe . . . today! In view of her relationship with Kennedy, speaking with Claudia Jeffries's new attorney posed some interesting problems.

"Hayley?"

She snapped her mind back to the present. "I'll call him right back. Thanks."

"Are you feeling all right?"

She heard the fatherly concern in his voice and railed at herself for being so unwrapped this morning. "I'm terrific, just feeling a little scattered. I hate being late."

He laughed. "Any particular reason you were?"

Hayley's hand tightened around the receiver. She felt like such a traitor that she had to compose herself before giving herself away and rushing to her own defense. "Lots of reasons," she admitted. "Probably too many to go into right now."

"Hmmm." Jason Sinclair's attention was already wandering to more pressing problems. "I'll leave Warren to you. If you need some help, give me a holler."

Hayley knew her father understood how grueling the whole Taft case had been for her—and still was—and his offer was not given lightly. Claudia Jeffries had been a difficult woman to work with, but Warren Smythe was not known for his tact, either. If Hayley'd been able to pick between the two, she would have chosen Claudia.

"Thank you," she said with humble sincerity. "I'll call Warren right away."

But after she hung up, her first thought was for Matthew Andrews. She still hadn't connected with him about Tom Wilson's reverse-discrimination suit.

Knowing she was motivated by pure cowardice, she called Smythe's office and left a message with his secretary explaining that she wouldn't be able to meet with him until the next day.

You're doing this because of Kennedy! she warned herself. *You're procrastinating for all the wrong reasons.*

She shook her head in frustration but didn't ring Smythe's office back. The deed was done, and she was honest enough to admit to being relieved.

Shaking out her raincoat, she hung it on the oak rack by the door, then touched a hand to her hair. She was surprised all the pins had stayed in place; she'd redone her chignon while literally on the run, Kennedy's sexy laughter following her out of her apartment.

She buzzed Matthew's office but received no answer. Smiling to herself, she reflected she wasn't the only one late to work that morning.

At the coffee machine she ran into Bernadette, the secretary who'd told her Matthew had left early the evening before. Petite, intelligent and fiery, Bernadette was known for having an ear to the ground when it came to office scuttlebutt. Hayley approached her with a certain amount of trepidation.

"I haven't seen Matthew this morning," Hayley remarked offhandedly. "Do you know if he's coming in today?"

Bernadette's black brows lifted a millimeter. "He should be here. You're still looking for him?"

With dark amusement, Hayley wondered if Bernadette was beginning to imagine a romance blooming between herself and Matthew. If only things were that simple!

"No. He's been a ghost around here since yesterday morning."

"Hmm. I haven't heard anything," Bernadette answered, looking piqued.

Some imp inside Hayley couldn't help asking, "Do you think he's avoiding me?"

"Impossible." On that point Bernadette was positive. "You're the only reason he comes to work at all."

Hayley opened her mouth to laugh, but Bernadette's reply had been in utter seriousness. The secretary filled her coffee cup and walked back to the humming memory typewriter centered in her circular workspace.

Several moments ticked by before Hayley filled her

own cup and headed back to her office. She didn't like the ideas Bernadette had unknowingly germinated. Matthew Andrews was in love with his wife, Sheryl. Hayley knew that. He'd certainly told her often enough, and his actions said the same. Yet, she also knew, with a woman's unerring feminine instinct, that if she were to give him any kind of sign that she was interested in more than friendship . . . well, she was aware, without ego, that Matthew might easily respond.

Feeling totally frustrated, Hayley shuffled through the correspondence on her desk, wishing she could just see Matthew and be done with it. She had the unshakable feeling of problems fermenting between them that could very well become insurmountable. And, completely ignoring logic, felt her relationship with Kennedy was somehow to blame.

How had life become so complicated? Before the Taft trial nothing had rippled the smooth surface of her life, but now? She seemed to be tiptoeing on eggshells every minute of the day.

The Cheswick's lobby was full of arriving guests; it was that time of day. Kennedy glanced impatiently at the long lines and headed for the two mahoghany-veneered elevators, stabbing the up button. He'd have to extend his reservation from the phone in his room.

But once in the opulent suite, his first move was to head straight for the shower and a change of clothes. A little surprised at his irrationality, he felt a growing eagerness to prepare for the evening ahead, an excitement that had been sorely missing from his life for a long, long time.

He hadn't lied when he'd told Hayley that he'd never felt about a woman the way he did about her. Even his marriage, colossal mistake that it was, had been based less on emotion and more on calculation— she'd seemed to be the right woman at the right time.

But this pleasure Hayley created, this seething anticipation, was something entirely new and foreign to him. It was probably even dangerous, he concluded, perfectly aware of how susceptible he'd become to her. Still, he was willing to take the risk.

He showered and dressed, allowing himself the luxury of concentrating solely on Hayley. Hayley. God! He could feel the first signals of arousal, a kind of pain mixed with pleasure, just thinking about her. It was baffling, and a little alarming, that his body could react so quickly. He was too old to be so influenced by his hormones, wasn't he? And too young—and rational, he reminded himself fiercely— to be having a mid-life crisis.

So what did that leave?

You're falling in love with her, pal.

Kennedy winced at the thought, not entirely sure he liked the idea. Being in love with her could have complications. There were things she'd said, things that had bothered him, things he'd purposely ignored when his prime interest had been to satisfy his need of her, to sink into her, drowning in the ecstacy of her.

But those things couldn't be ignored forever. And she'd been right when she'd said everything had a beginning . . . and an ending. . . .

Kennedy was toweling his hair dry when he saw the flashing red light on his telephone. Scowling, he threw down the towel and picked up the receiver, wondering if Hayley was suffering from a bad case of second thoughts.

Some inner sense warned him otherwise, the kind of scary intuition that one sometimes receives out of the blue. He replaced the receiver and stared at it, then strode to the bar and fixed himself a drink. It was more to buy himself some time than out of an actual desire for alcohol.

The second time he picked up the phone he called the desk. "Hello, this is Kennedy Taft, in 1421. There's a message for me."

"Just a minute." He was placed on hold, then the desk clerk clicked back on. "There are two messages, Mr. Taft. Both from Gordon Woodrow." He rattled off the number but Kennedy already knew it by heart.

"Thank you."

So, he thought darkly, dialing Gordon's number at Titan Pictures, his instincts had been right. Woodrow was too savvy; he'd known Kennedy's reasons for staying in Portland better than Kennedy had himself. And Gordon's reasons for objecting to his seeing Hayley were equally sound: Titan's own trial with Claudia Jeffries hadn't yet begun, and even though Hayley wasn't directly involved with the case an alliance between her and Kennedy would be news— the kind that could be blown way out of proportion. The publicity and rife speculation that could follow wouldn't be good for Titan Pictures.

Kennedy felt a burning frustration over the whole

thing. It shouldn't be any of their damned business, but rationally, he understood why it was.

"Hello, Gordon," he clipped out, when the studio executive came on the line. "What's up?"

"Ah, Kennedy. Still vacationing in gloomy Oregon? You sound like it."

Kennedy stifled his annoyance and managed a bland, "You should have stayed, Gordon."

"Is it still raining?"

"Yes."

"Then why," he asked deliberately, "would I want to be there?"

Kennedy could think of half a dozen reasons but wisely kept them to himself. Antagonizing Gordon wasn't something he really wanted to do. He liked Gordon Woodrow, though once in a while the man's narrow—and exceedingly shallow—tastes made him long for a more intellectual studio contact.

"How's the lady lawyer?" Gordon asked nonchalantly.

"Moving on to her next case, I'd imagine."

"You?" The lewdness in that one simple word made Kennedy's jaw tighten. "Well, I hate to spoil the honeymoon," Gordon went on, unruffled by the angry sound from the other end of the line, "but you're needed back in sunny California."

"What for?" Kennedy demanded suspiciously.

"*Pleasure Hunt,* pal. Remember that one? Production's moved up and we're going to start as soon as you roll into town."

Kennedy clapped his hand to the back of his neck, stunned by the suddenness of Titan's decision. *Pleas-*

ure Hunt, an adventure comedy concerning a world-wide scavenger hunt among the wealthiest people on earth, had been slated to begin production the following month. Kennedy had accepted the job of director with mixed feelings—it wasn't really his type of movie, but his salary offer, and profit percentages, had been staggering. Now, however, he wished he'd refused.

The picture was being shot at several different exotic locales; it would take him away from Hayley for months.

"Gordon," he said softly, his head throbbing. He felt himself being sucked beneath a powerful undertow. He was powerless, helpless. "I can't do it."

A pregnant pause, full of hostility, ensued. "Now, why did I know you were going to say that?" Gordon asked with deceptive calmness.

"Because you've guessed how I feel about Hayley Sinclair," Kennedy answered grimly. The issue was plain now. Deception was out of the question.

"Damn it, Kennedy! What's gotten into you? If you want women, get back here. This picture's got more famous, gorgeous torsos than all the films you've made in your entire lifetime!"

Kennedy's mind was flashing ahead, speeding toward a granite wall of unacceptable conclusions. Hayley would never forgive him for leaving now. It would be breaking the dam before the first crack was even discovered. "It's not women, Gordon. It's woman. As in singular. And I'm interested in a little more than torsos."

"There are an awful lot of nice faces too, pal. They could make a man stop breathing."

Kennedy's mouth twisted at Gordon's irrepressibility. "I need to breathe if I'm going to work," he pointed out dryly. Then, because he truly wanted Gordon to understand, he added, "There are such things as intelligence, and respect, and admiration, that are far more captivating. Just the wrapping isn't going to cut it anymore. I want the whole package."

"Oh, no," Gordon groaned. "You've got it bad, my friend. And you picked the wrong lady."

Kennedy didn't argue with him. He was already too aware of the problems between himself and Hayley. But given a little time, he was convinced they could all be smoothed over. And to his way of thinking, the wait was worth the end result: the *chance* to be with Hayley . . . maybe even permanently.

"But you can't get out of this contract, Kennedy. You're locked in too tightly."

It was a warning from a friend, not a threat from a Titan executive. Shoulders slumping in defeat, Kennedy knew Gordon was absolutely right. A contract dispute with the studio would be bloody, and he would end up the loser.

"I need a little time, Gordon."

"You don't have time! Haven't you been listening to anything I've said?"

"Oh, I've heard you." Kennedy focused his gaze unseeingly out the window of his suite, upon the unbroken gray cloud cover. Gray sky, gray buildings, gray water . . . gray like Hayley's eyes.

"Listen." Gordon's voice changed, a drop in decibel level that nevertheless became more penetrating. "I know how you feel. You're in the first throes of an all-consuming love affair."

Kennedy's brows descended. This didn't sound like the Gordon he knew, and he didn't like what he was hearing.

"It's passionate. It's glorious. It's probably all you can think about."

"I'm thirty-eight," Kennedy cut in swiftly. He was astonished and annoyed by Gordon's presumption that he didn't know his own mind.

"What the hell does that matter? You've finally found a woman who interests you! And believe me, pal, as much as I think you're making a mistake, it's nice to know it's finally happened."

Kennedy had had about all he could take. "I'll call you back tomorrow."

"Tonight." Gordon was firm.

"Tomorrow." Kennedy was firmer.

"Think about what I've said, huh?"

Kennedy made a gruff noise of acquiescence and slammed the phone into its cradle. He was totally, insensibly furious. He raked his fingers through the wiry thickness of his hair and realized it was an action he'd repeated at least a dozen times already.

"Damn!"

He seriously considered calling Hayley, now, while the problem was still fresh, still as seemingly impossible to him as it would be to her when he hit her with it. But he was tired of the telephone, and even more tired of problems that shouldn't have been problems at all.

Cradling his drink, he tried to lock his emotions in a separate part of his mind and think rationally and systematically. His relationship with Hayley—exciting and tempting as it was—was as nebulous and rocky as it had been from the first moment he'd laid eyes on her. Nothing had changed. Nothing, except that they'd tapped into a deep-rooted need that each one of them had, yet hadn't known they possessed.

But what was that? Anything? Everything? *Nothing?*

Just where do you expect this relationship to go?

Unbidden memories of Hayley tumbled into his thoughts: her smooth skin, the vulnerability behind her eyes, her regal cheekbones, the slow smile that prefaced each self-mocking comment. . . . God. Kennedy closed his eyes, exhausted by trying to keep those potent emotions at bay.

He downed his drink in one motion. If it took anesthetizing himself, so be it. He was going to have to come up with a solution before he laid out the problem to Hayley. Either that, or face the fact that he might lose her. And Kennedy was a very poor loser indeed.

Chapter Seven

The bags of groceries she carried up the walk tilted crazily, and Hayley tried to move slowly and carefully though she felt the numbness in her fingers growing by the second.

The rain had cleared, but an invading chill had settled over the city, freezing all parts of one's body that weren't covered. Hayley's nose tingled; the nyloned tips of her toes, peeking out from navy heels, had no feeling whatsoever. But the cold front had swept away the cloud cover, turning the night into a million diamond-clear lights and stars, spangled and dazzling against a black velvet sky.

She knocked at her own door, holding her breath. What if he wasn't there? What if all that feeling, all that love they'd shared, was self-conceived? Kennedy hadn't called her all day, though he'd never said he would. She'd thought about calling him a time or two but had felt that was being too possessive.

Now, waiting for an answer, paralyzed with uncertainty, Hayley considered the fact that he might have easily just caught the next flight out of town. No good-byes. No regrets. She closed her eyes against the shattering scenario, hating herself for her doubts.

The door swung inward and suddenly Kennedy was lifting the bags from her cold-stiffened arms. "Why didn't you tell me you had all these?" he demanded, shifting the weight of the groceries easily. "I would have carried them up. Are there any more?" His silver-green eyes peered at her closely. "Are you all right?" he asked a trifle grimly, seeing her pale face and widened eyes.

"Of course. Just a little cold." Hayley's eyes turned to the fireplace. Flames were sizzling with burning pitch and she moved gratefully toward the warmth, swallowing her relief. So much for thinking he'd run out on her. She chided herself for caring so much— too much.

She jumped when Kennedy came up behind her, his hands fishing the pins from her hair.

"Hmm. You are cold," he murmured, his lips touching the back of her nape.

"It's cold out there," Hayley said, trembling a little, thinking she needed a harder shell where this man was concerned. "The weather's changed. Really unusual. It doesn't generally get this cold until December, or maybe after the first of the year, that is if it gets this cold at all. . . ."

She was babbling. Realizing it, Hayley fell into an

uncomfortable silence, wishing Kennedy didn't have the unique knack for making her feel awkward.

Kennedy's brow furrowed as he sensed her mood. He didn't make any more obviously untoward advances, though it took a good deal of restraint to keep his hands to himself. Jamming his fists deep inside the pockets of his slightly faded jeans, Kennedy wondered if he'd been too familiar, taken too many things for granted. Maybe he'd dropped formality too quickly. Hayley was as nervous as a cat.

"What's wrong?" he asked quietly.

Her back was to him and she lifted her shoulders tensely. "Nothing's wrong. I just thought you might . . ." Hayley linked her fingers together and concentrated on the flames. It was so hard to say exactly what she felt, when every word might come back to haunt her, mock her. ". . . have had a change of plans."

"Change of plans?"

She heard the quickening of his voice and was stabbed with the knowledge that she'd been right! Her throat was suddenly hot and dry, squeezing off her air.

"What do you mean 'a change of plans'?" Kennedy demanded again. His hands gripped her shoulders, turning her to face him. He was stunned. How could she know already?

"You're leaving, aren't you?"

The accusatory tilt of her chin defeated him. "Not tonight," he said. Her eyes flashed at his prevarication. Kennedy ran his hand around the back of his neck and admitted wearily, "Soon though." Then, he asked, "How did you know?"

Hayley attempted a lightness that didn't quite come off. "Oh, I think it was self-evident. It would be harder to believe that you were staying."

"Hayley—"

"No." She twisted from his hands, unable to hear the platitudes that were bound to come. And she'd known it! She'd *known* it! She just hadn't expected the break to come so soon.

Kennedy was thrown off-balance. He wasn't used to having situations out of his control, but Hayley had battered his explanations before he'd even had a chance to give them.

"Would you like a cup of coffee? I think I need a cup to take the chill off." Hayley was already heading to the kitchen, her back painfully rigid, as if she'd just inhaled a huge lungful of air and refused to let it out.

"Damn it, Hayley."

He wheeled her around before she reached the kitchen archway, soft fury radiating from his voice. She wanted to fight, but his steel strength was unbeatable. She crumpled against his chest, his taut voice ringing in her ears.

"I don't know how you read me so well, but you've got the message all wrong. Yes, I have to leave. I've got a picture—a contract—that I can't get out of."

"It doesn't matter." Hayley didn't care what the excuse was.

"The hell it doesn't!"

If she'd had time, she supposed later she would

have been frightened. Kennedy's intensity took her breath away. But he pushed her to arm's length, just far enough to see every emotion on her face without letting her go.

"I should have gone today. Hell, I should've gone yesterday. But I stayed because the plain truth is, I can't get you off my mind. Last night—"

Hayley shrank within herself. She didn't want to think about last night.

Kennedy controlled the urge to shake some sense into her. "Last night," he said again, deliberately, staring down the cool distrust in her gray eyes, "was beautiful. Deny that, if you can."

Hayley's mouth quivered, anxious to deny, to save herself exhausting, unavoidable pain. But she couldn't deny it, and Kennedy knew it. "I'm not like you," she whispered. "I can't just go on, knowing the end's coming, blithely ignoring it. I don't work that way. Kennedy, please . . ."

"Oh, Hayley. God. You don't give yourself a chance."

His anguish was worse than his anger. She turned her face toward the darkened hallway to her bedroom. "I'd rather deal with my feelings now and be done with it." Her hands moved in beseeching circles. "I can't—just put this—on hold."

"And I can't just give up, love. I'm not leaving forever, ya know."

Hayley kept her eyes trained away from his. "How long will you be gone, Kennedy? How long before I see you again?"

He hadn't expected her to tackle that issue so soon. His lips tightened. "I don't know," he said testily.

Her chin rotated slowly back, her gray eyes worldly-wise and weary. "Checkmate."

Kennedy gritted his teeth. He knew better than to go into a long dissertation about the movie he was bound to. It would come off sounding like a feeble excuse. "If I'm lucky, I can catch a weekend or two within the next few months. If I'm not, then I won't be able to get away until after production's complete—three or four months."

Hayley knew, even if he didn't yet, that it would never work. "Don't give me false hope, Kennedy," she pleaded softly. "Don't make it any worse on me."

His hands crept to her nape, thumbs trailing her jaw. "Don't be such a pessimist, sweetheart," he returned, mouth quirking sensually. "Things will work out."

She wished she had his unfailing belief in the future, but all she could think about was the sorrowful past.

Yet he was tantalizing her into forgetting.

"I—"

Hayley caught her breath as his lips brushed her mouth, lean hips and thighs backing her against the wall, sapping her strength to fight.

She closed her eyes and whimpered, "I'm not ready for this."

"You weren't ready last night either."

"I'm going to hurt. I'm going to hurt so bad."

Her fear wrenched at Kennedy's heart. "I wouldn't hurt you. I couldn't," he grated fiercely.

Her head was moving back and forth in tortuous denial, her hair a wild, sun-streaked flurry.

"Forget about that ex-husband of yours," he said tautly. "If you'd never met him, would you be so scared to try again?"

His thighs were rigid against her legs. Hayley felt their pressure keenly. "Maybe. Probably."

"Liar."

His weight fell against hers, but in a thrilling, thrilling way. She was weak, immobilized and totally at his mercy when he ground against her in wide, slow circles. Her hands slid to his hips in a vain effort to stop him, but they just rested there, unable to do anything to halt his sweet torment.

His mouth was on the downy angle of her jaw. "Don't give up on us so easily, Hayley," he urged. "There's too much to lose."

She squeezed her eyes shut. "I don't want to. . . ."

It was her strong need for self-preservation that made her, but Kennedy's movements were blowing caution to the four winds.

His lips captured hers and Hayley lifted her arms to wind around his neck, her fingers burrowing into his thick hair. Her mind blurred. She couldn't remember what she was fighting.

"I love you, Hayley," he murmured.

She shook her head, but his mouth had found hers again, devising new ways to crumble her resistance. His tongue touched and twisted, and his hands found all her secret places, until Hayley melted into silk in his arms.

She told herself, as Kennedy scooped her to him,

lifting her with ease, that believing those three little words had been the downfall of more than one woman. But none of it seemed to matter as he kicked the door to her bedroom closed, his eyes surveying her with a burning impatience that fired something primal in her blood.

"I'm procrastinating again," she said mindlessly, feeling his hands tremble slightly as he stripped off her clothes.

"No, no." His naked body covered hers, warm and heated and taut with desire.

"Just tonight," she said, shuddering as his tongue licked against her breasts. She was restless and eager, responding with a moan as his fingers gently invaded her.

He didn't argue with her; there was no point in lying. And after that he forgot everything as Hayley pulled him down to her, passion making her bold, her hands and body making it impossible for him to keep his head.

At the searing moment of union he told her again, teeth gritted, "I love you, Hayley. Love you . . ." Then the world turned into a glowing, bursting orb, and sensation after honeyed sensation ravaged his body as Hayley reached that spinning ecstacy at the same timeless moment.

"Good afternoon, Hayley."

The door to the conference room swung slowly shut behind her, clicking softly as Hayley managed a brittle smile for Warren Smythe. Inside, she was strung tight as a bowstring, hurting, her whole being consumed by a dull, persistent ache. It was not the hurt that was yet to come, the hurt that would blind her when she got home and found herself alone, but it was bad enough, a physical "I told you so" that made each minute of the day drag an eternity.

She'd left for work that morning without saying good-bye. Kennedy had made no promises about seeing her again; Hayley hadn't asked for any. It seemed simpler just to walk out than fuss over an embarrassed "we'll meet again sometime," a situation she knew she couldn't have handled without breaking down in some unforgivable way.

And so she'd suffered through an intolerable morning of normality, her brave facade never cracking. She was determined not to let her emotions affect the quality of her work. But it was a strain—one that had only intensified when she'd been informed that Warren Smythe was waiting to speak to her.

"Nice to see you again, Warren," Hayley replied, walking toward the conference table and accepting his outstretched hand. Perspiration gathered in the valley between her breasts. She'd hoped—foolishly, she now realized—that by the time she met with Warren her relationship with Kennedy would have cooled.

It has, at least on his side, she brutally reminded herself.

Warren was dressed in a three-piece, expensive designer suit of smoky gray. His brown hair was thinning; a downy tuft had been islanded on his forehead. But he was still arrogantly handsome, and had used his stunning appearance to best advantage in more than one courtroom.

His hand covered a manila folder, the beautifully manicured fingers eclipsed by a fabulous, glinting ruby adorning his ring finger. Business had been good for Warren Smythe for a long, long time.

"Okay," he said, frowning as Hayley sat across from him. The table was wide and circular, and though she supposed it would have made more sense to sit next to him, Hayley couldn't bring herself to do it. She disliked the man on principle.

"I've got a few questions about Taft," he said, smoothing his vest. "More than a few, actually."

Hayley's pulse leaped, but she nodded. *He doesn't know,* she reminded herself firmly. "Go ahead."

"Let's go back to the deposition." He carefully turned over several pages in the folder. "I've got the words here, but I want your impression of Taft as a person."

"My impression?" Hayley repeated slowly. This was hardly the kind of question normally asked between attorneys. And Warren especially was almost compulsive about sticking to facts.

Warren sighed in noisy impatience. "Did he strike you as a man who would lie? Maybe even on the witness stand?"

"No!" Startled, Hayley's lips tightened in affront. "You're talking about perjury, Warren. A criminal offense. Mr. Taft's too smart, and has too much integrity, to commit perjury."

She felt anger seethe beneath her skin. It was one thing to find reason for an appeal through some minor error made during the trial, quite another to point an accusing finger at the validity of the defendant's testimony—that had already been decided by the jury.

"You're awfully sure of yourself, Hayley. Did you gain this impression during the deposition, or while you were in court?" He looked only mildly interested in her answer. "Or—"Warren absently fingered the typewritten deposition—"was this something you decided after the trial?"

Hayley knew enough about Warren's tactics to hang onto her temper. "What are you implying?" she asked coldly.

"I'm not implying anything. I'm just asking."

Hayley drew in a calming breath. Warren Smythe was too calculating for his own good. "Kennedy Taft strikes me as the kind of man who wouldn't save his own neck at the expense of others," she said levelly. "He wouldn't lie to cover up mistakes. He's straightforward, and doesn't falter when the questions get tough. He impressed me, Warren, but more importantly, he impressed the jury."

"That's why you think you lost?"

"Partially," Hayley conceded. "But the facts spoke for themselves too. Claudia didn't have a strong enough case."

Warren looked thoughtful. "So you think an appeal wouldn't do much good."

Hayley was about to agree, then hastily made a quick reassessment of her feelings. She wasn't purposely deflecting Warren because she cared about Kennedy, was she? No matter that it was over between herself and Kennedy, she still loved him. Was that love poisoning her reason? Was she trying to sandbag Claudia Jeffries's attempts to appeal? A woman who'd counted on Hayley to present a fair case against Kennedy Taft?

And what about Lisa Jeffries, age nine?

"I don't know what to think," Hayley said through tight lips, her heated introspection bringing unwanted color to her cheeks.

Warren Smythe's eyes narrowed. He was the kind of man who could practically smell when another person wasn't telling the complete truth, and Hayley Sinclair was sidestepping all over the place.

With a feeling of smug satisfaction, he briskly flipped through several more pages. "Okay, Hayley, let's get down to the events of the trial. I have a transcript right here. Let's take it from the top . . . hmm?"

Three hours later Hayley was released from the conference room, a room that had taken on a new dimension as far as she was concerned. It was more like a confessional or an interrogation room now; she didn't want ever to set foot inside it again.

Warren hadn't been satisfied with her answers, and Hayley knew why. They were quick, concise and sorely lacking in personal prejudice—the way Hayley instructed her clients to respond on the witness stand.

The trouble was, Warren Smythe was fishing for much, much more. And Hayley was concerned because she wasn't exactly sure what that "much more" might be. It was almost as if he *knew* how she felt about Kennedy, and was just trying to trap her into admitting it.

"I'm going to want to talk to you again," he'd said, snapping his briefcase closed with imperative decision. "Soon. I want my presentation to the State Court of Appeals made by the end of next week." His eye had traveled over her drawn features with tireless intensity. "But you look like you've had enough for one day."

Hayley had battled valiantly for hours. She'd smiled vaguely, and asked, "Haven't you? We've both put in a pretty full afternoon."

Warren's face had clouded, as if he couldn't quite figure her out. "How about another meeting Friday? I'll go over what we discussed and see if there's something I've missed."

Hayley had been relieved to end the discussion, and had left Warren with a perfunctory "Good luck," before walking past an interested Bernadette on the way back to her office.

Once inside, she'd collapsed against the haven of her door. Her deception—for that's what it was beginning to become—over Kennedy was taking a toll she'd been too naive at first to appreciate. Now, she worried her bottom lip and wondered if she should have told Warren the truth. He might have been less hard on her, or, at the very least, enlightened to her ambivalence.

On the other hand, he could have made the situation unbearably embarrassing for her and Kennedy.

She agonized for several minutes about calling her father, picking up the phone twice, then slamming it down as many times. Pressing her palm hard against her cheek, Hayley tried to dissolve her worries ration-

ally. Was she making too much of Warren's insinua-
tive comments? Was she, as Kennedy had intimated,
always expecting the worst? Was her own guilt eating
her up inside, causing her to lose the one thing she
prided herself most on, her perspective?

And what does it matter, anyway? she asked herself
angrily. *It's over.* No surprise, certainly, just a de-
pressing reality that had turned her world topsy-turvy.
But if she reached way down deep, into the heart of
her feelings, she knew there was an ember of hope
that stubbornly refused to die, one that desperately
wanted to believe everything Kennedy proposed . . .
and that was what worried her most of all.

Hayley was gathering up her coat to leave when she
heard the unmistakable sound of Matthew Andrews's
voice. She quickly dropped everything and headed in
the direction of his office, receiving a nod from
Bernadette as she raised her eyebrows and cocked her
head in the direction of Matthew's office.

Matthew's door was ajar, and Hayley could hear
him on the phone. She hesitated, her hand raised to
knock, an unwilling eavesdropper to part of a disturbing conversation.

". . . I'm trying," Matthew was saying urgently,
"but you've got to give me a little more time." He
swore beneath his breath, adding harshly, "I'm *not*
losing control. Just a little while longer, everything'll
be just as it was before. I promise." A pause, then a
deep sigh. "I know. They're trying to take the case
away from me. . . ."

The bitterness of Matthew's tone chilled Hayley's

blood. Her mouth turned down in unhappiness. She'd known this was going to happen.

Hayley rapped loudly, poking her head through the opening between his door and the wall. Matthew's anger was swiftly replaced by another violent emotion, and with a terse, "I'll call you later," he slammed down the phone, glaring at Hayley.

Hayley raised her palms in mock surrender. "I couldn't help overhearing," she apologized.

"Couldn't help?" His voice was heavy with sarcasm.

"Look, I've been trying to reach you for two days, but you weren't here."

Matthew took a deep breath and swept a tired hand through his hair. "That's right. I took a mini-vacation. Some well-deserved time off. Sinclair, Holmsby, and Layton doesn't need me around anyway."

"Oh, Matthew. That's not true." As bad as she felt, Hayley couldn't let him wallow in self-pity.

Matthew's shoulders squared defiantly. "Was there something specific you wanted to say?"

"I'm sorry about the Wilson case. I didn't want things to turn out this way."

Matthew's mouth was thin as a blade. "Was it your father's decision?"

Hayley tried to keep her shoulders from slumping. As if the day hadn't been long enough already. "You know it was."

"Uh-huh."

His finality infuriated Hayley; the underlying message that her father was giving her, as usual, preferential treatment, fanned her smoldering resentment. She debated on telling him all the reasons why she was the better choice for the reverse-discrimination suit, but in the end said nothing. Matthew, when he finished licking his wounds, would figure it out.

"How was Sheryl?" she asked, after a few minutes of silence.

"Sheryl?"

"You were talking to her on the phone, weren't you?" It had been Hayley's natural assumption that Sheryl was on the other end of that conversation. She'd come to know the urgent anxiety that threaded through Matthew's voice whenever he spoke to, or about, his wife, and she didn't see who else it could possibly be.

Matthew frowned, then muttered, "Oh . . . yeah . . . she's just the same as always. I'd probably do well to forget her." A semblance of his old smile crossed his face. "Sorry I came down on you. The Wilson case—"he shrugged in forgiveness—"it doesn't much matter anyway."

"Come on, Matthew."

He scrubbed his face tiredly with his palm. "No, I mean it, Hayley. It's not that important. I don't want to blow it with you too."

Hayley smiled. "You can't," she assured him. She wasn't in the least fooled by Matthew's amateurish attempts at nonchalance. He was hurting.

"Is there anything I can do?" Hayley added, her heartfelt words enough to make Matthew wince.

He managed a sad, defeated smile. "No. It's just

one more minor crisis in the midst of thousands. I'm gonna chalk this year up to the worst in my life. How are you doing?"

A tough question. Hayley marked time for half a beat before asking, "Are we talking professionally, or personally?"

"Are you seeing Kennedy Taft?"

Hayley's head jerked, her eyes widening in surprise. She had a string of half-truths already hovering on her tongue when she saw the look on Matthew's face. He knew.

Her hesitation was packed with guilt. "I was," she admitted quietly, folding her arms protectively beneath her breasts. She tried to add, *He's gone now. Out of my life. Probably winging his way back to Hollywood as we speak. . . .*

But she couldn't say anything. She didn't know it, but her face said it all—the tiny fissures in her brave mask breaking open all at once. She felt as if a cold hand had closed around her heart.

Matthew raised skeptical eyebrows. "Chancy," was all he said.

"Worse than chancy," Hayley agreed dully. She walked to the window and tried to ignore the doleful shaking of Matthew's head.

"I don't want to bring you down. But, Hayley, was it worth the risk?"

There's an element of risk in everything.

Hayley knotted her hands together. "Only time will tell," she muttered with false brightness. Anyway, it doesn't matter anymore." She laughed a trifle shakily. "Who knows why we do the things we do, Matthew."

Matthew's silence penetrated her brain, and Hayley turned, catching the harsh tension in his face, his balled fists. When he realized she was watching him, he sighed, slowly loosening his hands. "Well, I hope you have better luck with your love life than I've had with mine. Rejection's pure hell."

It was Matt's last declaration that hung heavy in her thoughts while she retraced her steps to her office. He was so horribly right. It was rejection that she had feared more than anything—Kennedy's rejection. And it had come in the guise of an important movie assignment. Certainly more subtle than Sheryl Andrews's demand of a divorce, it was nevertheless the first step toward ending their relationship before it had even begun.

And it was painful. She ached all over.

Hayley was slipping her arms into her raincoat and reaching for her purse when Matthew suddenly appeared at her door. "I've got my notes on the Wilson case," he explained, waving the file like a white flag. "Thought I'd drop 'em by now."

"You're one in a million, Matt," Hayley said, smiling her relief. Her phone buzzed before she could say anything more, but she signaled Matthew to stay as she picked up the receiver. She wanted the whole tender issue of the Wilson case completely understood, then forgotten. With everything else going wrong, she wasn't going to risk her friendship with Matt too.

"Hello?"

"Hello, counselor." Kennedy's voice was a sexy, disturbing drawl.

Hayley's lips parted, delight shimmering through her with the swiftness of a summer storm. For a moment she could say nothing at all. Then, she asked with controlled carefulness, "Well, hello. Are you— still in town?"

Matthew was standing at strict attention. One glance at Hayley's changing expression and he walked to her desk, placing the file neatly in the center before giving her a long, considering look. Intriguing color was creeping up her neck, flushing her face, brightening her eyes. He drew a heavy sigh, closing the office door softly behind him on his way out.

Hayley turned at the sound, but was compelled back to the phone by Kennedy's answer.

"I'm here for the rest of the week," he told her. "I'm sure Gordon will hog-tie, tar and feather me when I get back but I don't much care. I've got a reprieve, love. Three whole days. Let's make this thing between us work before circumstances beyond our control pull us apart."

Hayley desperately tried to bank down her jubilation. She smothered her relief under a repressing, "I'd be crazy to go any further with you, Kennedy."

"Then be crazy. Say yes."

She was smiling. She couldn't help herself. "Yes to what?"

"Yes to 'Will you meet me at the Cheswick for dinner?' Yes to 'Have you gotten over all those ridiculous fears about me?' Yes to 'Do you love me?' "

"You're impossible," she answered, laughing.

"Am I?"

"Yes."

She heard his silent laughter. "And I love you too," he whispered, a half second before she realized how he'd interpreted her.

The telephone disconnected with a satisfied-sounding click.

Chapter Eight

The Cheswick Hotel boasted a string quartet in its lobby restaurant Wednesdays through Saturdays. Hayley heard the muted throbbing sounds of the bass fiddle, counterpoint to the sweet melancholy of the violin, as she pushed her palms against the magnificent doors from the underground lot.

People were standing in the lobby in informal groups, some waiting patiently at the foot of the half flight of blood-red-carpeted stairs that led to the restaurant. The maître d' was checking his list, illumination provided by a small brass lamp with a green shade. He nodded benignly to an elegant couple, then led them to their table.

Kennedy was standing to one side. Before Hayley had time to feel like a woman alone, he walked in easy strides across the length of the room, his flashing smile weakening what paltry resistance she had left.

"I thought you might get cold feet at the last minute," he said, tucking her hand inside his arm.

Hayley smiled. "I said I'd be here . . . I think."

They both laughed.

"You said a lot of things, as I recall," Kennedy reminded her in a tone that was just short of being smug.

Hayley felt too good to rise to the bait. She shot him a sidelong glance. "That's not how I remember the conversation."

"How do you remember it?" He met her gaze with one smoldering with entirely different messages, messages that burned through her veins, making her feel gloriously dizzy.

There was no use denying what they both knew. "Well, I didn't say no."

"Hmm. Don't think that word's in my vocabulary," Kennedy rubbed his nose thoughtfully. "How do you spell it?"

"N-O-E."

Kennedy's laugh came straight from his chest, low and rolling and utterly irresistible. "Good thing you're a better lawyer than speller," he whispered in her ear as the maître d' led them to their table.

A half wall topped with an etched-glass window offered some privacy for their table. Hayley barely noticed. As far as she was concerned the setting didn't matter—as long as she was with Kennedy.

A far cry from your dismal thoughts of this morning, she reminded herself.

"What are you thinking about?" Kennedy asked, seeing the wisp of regret slide across her smooth features.

"You, mostly. Me, some." Hayley inhaled the delicate scent of amaretto from her steaming cup of coffee. "This morning I thought I walked out on you forever."

Kennedy shook his head slowly from side to side, his eyes never leaving hers. "It's not going to be that easy, love." Determination was stamped on his chin as he added softly, "I won't let it be."

Hayley said nothing, immersed in dangerous thoughts of love and commitment. Kennedy eased her hands from cupping her drink, holding them tightly between his capable palms.

"This thing between us, Hayley. The way I feel." His low-timbred voice was even lower, the tones lifting the hair on her arms, quickening her pulse. "It's something I can't give up on. Do you understand that?"

She was beginning to. God. She *wanted* to! And with each passing moment she was drawing closer to believing every beautiful hope and dream that he did. It was like the slow opening of a heavy door; she was trembling with anticipation, afraid and fascinated by what lay beyond.

Kennedy frowned, his face tense and serious. "You scare me, Hayley. I'm not used to feeling this way."

Hayley swallowed hard. "Neither am I," she admitted in a barely audible voice.

"This may be a once-in-a-lifetime thing."

Hayley was bursting inside, her lungs expanding

until she felt faint with lack of air. She couldn't listen to him. She had to! There was nowhere for them to go from here. There was the whole untouched, shining future ahead. He'd promised her nothing. He'd given her a whole new world.

"We're both too wise to believe that," she murmured, trembling.

"What are you so afraid of?"

"You!" Hayley's eyes met his squarely. "Oh, Kennedy. You make it so hard to be sane."

The worry that had creased his forehead disappeared. "I love you," he said, giving her no chance to avoid his all-seeing eyes.

He wasn't asking her, but she knew it was the time to say it back. *I love you.* It would be so easy because it was the absolute truth.

She stared at him, the moment spinning out like a drugging spell. The words hung, unspoken, between them, but as Hayley formed them in her mind she was seized by an unreasonable panic. She was setting herself up for the most brutal kind of pain imaginable! She could only gaze at him mutely, feeling anguished that she couldn't give him such a simple security.

Kennedy sat back wearily, sensing he'd lost something he might never find again.

"We've both been through unhappy marriages," Hayley said, trying to explain herself. "I can't just give in to—urges—that might not stand the test of time."

Kennedy's lips thinned in disgust. "You can't give in at all, Hayley. You're as cold and stiff as stone." His glance caught the flash of hurt that crossed her face. "But not always," he added in somber, seductive tones. "Sometimes you're hot, my love."

Hayley's neck snapped upward, eyes flickering wildly around the room, hands trembling between his. "Don't," she murmured.

"I can't help myself. You force me to do the most drastic things."

She wriggled one hand free but the other was well and truly captured. Her wrist was shackled by viselike fingers. Watching helplessly, Hayley saw Kennedy's head descend to her imprisoned palm.

His tongue touched its center. Nerves awakened with a shock. Hayley watched in frozen fascination as his tongue moved a small, intimate circle against her sensitized flesh.

"Give in," he murmured.

Hayley laughed shakily. "You don't ask for much, do you?"

"Just everything. And I'm not as confident as I look. Give in before my ego's shattered forever."

Hayley leaned her head weakly against the cushion, all feeling radiating from the center of her captured palm. "I think you'll survive. It's me I'm worried about."

"You worry too much."

"I have a lot to worry about."

Kennedy lifted his eyes to hers. "Would you worry less if I was out of your life completely?"

Hayley heard the important question hidden inside his words: *Do you want me to leave?* Suddenly she was standing at the crossroads of her future, a momentous decision waiting to be answered by one simple word.

"No," she said, placing her other hand over the tanned back of his.

Kennedy leaned forward, touching her lips to his, relief softening the hard line of his shoulders. Tiny kisses whispered against the corners of her mouth, the parted curve of her lips.

"How do you spell that?" he murmured, returning her smile.

"Y-E-S." She drew a wispy breath, gathering courage, then took the plunge. "As in I love you."

The look on his face made the risk worth it. She melted beneath his relieved grin. "Well, lady," he said on a delighted sigh, "it sure took you long enough to decide."

Hayley lowered her head, offering him a view of her now gently falling chignon. "Some decisions can't be made lightly."

His finger mapped one of the sun-streaked tresses that wove through her hair, fishing out the first of her pins. "You're so careful, love. Sometimes too careful. I never expected to find a woman who mattered to me this much. And then to find her unwilling . . . God." He pretended to shudder. "I may never be the same."

She vainly tried to stop his marauding hand but her hair was tumbling around her face in wild, burnished-gold beauty. "Stop that," she said without conviction.

"It was coming down anyway." He had the audacity to draw one honey-dipped strand across his lips. "Come here. I want to tell you something."

Hayley obediently leaned forward, her eyes wary. "If we're going to eat dinner here you're going to have to behave. Pretty soon I'll be hiding my face."

"Hmm . . . you smell good." He let out a supremely satisfied breath. "Don't worry. These people look like they need something to gossip about."

"You and I are a pretty good topic," Hayley reminded him. "The trial was only a few days ago."

Kennedy's face was very close to hers. Lips nearly touching her ear, he started saying the most wickedly erotic things that a man had ever said to her. Hayley blushed, divided between laughter and embarrassment. It seemed almost sinful to be listening to him while other people, old dowagers and businessmen, female executives and young couples, waiters, musicians, everyone floating through the lobby, were so close by. But it was terrific, and Hayley recognized the magic she'd been missing from her life. Quiet laughter spilled from her, and she bent her head. His chuckle was practically obscene.

She was just about to beg him to get her out of the restaurant and make good on his promises, when a pair of determined black high heels strode into her line of vision, stopping sharply at their table.

Hayley jerked back from Kennedy as if burned, her stomach filling with dread as her eyes encountered the dark fury simmering in Claudia Jeffries's.

"Hello, Miss Sinclair." Her head swiveled to Kennedy. "Mr. Taft." The emphasis was withering. "So this is why I lost my case."

It took several seconds before time seemed to resume for Hayley. Her shock was total. Then she heard Claudia's terrible insinuation.

Hayley half rose from her chair. "Claudia—" She

stared at the stylish woman blankly. She could think of absolutely nothing to say.

"I wouldn't jump to conclusions, Mrs. Jeffries." Kennedy was on his feet, addressing her with shocking calm.

"Jump to conclusions! I knew from the moment Miss Sinclair here took my case that I was being had." Claudia's pinched face accused Hayley of horrible transgressions. "Second rate. That's what you are. It's so much easier to lose a case than win one, right? God, you make me sick!"

Hayley gasped. Terrible fury darkened Kennedy's face. "You'd better be careful how you throw around accusations," he warned dangerously.

Hayley's insides were ravaged by quaking tremors. "Claudia, I tried to win for you," she said in a strange, disembodied voice.

"Sure you did." Claudia's lip curled into a snarl of disgust. "That's what this little tryst is all about. Well, you listen closely, Miss Sinclair. I've had a feeling about you all along." She glanced warily at Kennedy's threatening, silent form, then went on, "You've been sabotaging my case from the beginning. How much did he pay you? As much as I did? Did you get twice your expected fee, Miss Sinclair? Or was it more . . . ?"

"I've done nothing wrong." Hayley's voice was careful. It had to be. She was crying underneath.

"Get out of here before I throw you out."

Claudia's face whitened, mouth dropping in affront. Kennedy's terse threat made her lips tighten in fury. She made a strangled sound and, with an effort, swallowed back what she was going to say. She had never been a stupid woman.

"I'll sue you for misrepresentation," she hissed at Hayley. "You'll hear from *my* lawyer, Miss Attorney-at-Law."

Kennedy made a shifting move, an uneasy readying for battle. Claudia, understanding the significance implicitly, spun away after delivering Hayley one more strippingly hateful glare.

The restaurant seemed incredibly quiet, the violin sounding far away, filled with a haunted, empty sadness.

"Hayley—" Kennedy's face was grooved with concern.

Hayley couldn't see him through the dazed shock that disoriented her. She'd never witnessed such anger, such viciousness—and all directed at her! The weight in her stomach made her wonder if she might be physically sick.

"Hayley, love . . ." Kennedy wanted to reach out and drag her to the comfort of his arms, but he recognized her inner shrinking. He couldn't touch her yet.

"Don't listen to her," he begged softly, his chest filling with dreadful pain at the horror on her face. "She tried to hurt you where it would hurt the worst."

"I would never do that," she said blankly.

"I know. I know. And she knows it too. She just wanted to lash out at someone, and there you were." Kennedy's fingers curled into a shaking fist. "God, I could kill her for this!"

The explosion of his anger brought Hayley out of her daze. She stood up, her legs like rubber.

"Sit down," Kennedy urged gently.

"No, I have to leave."

"What? Where are you going?"

Tears were swimming behind her eyes. She felt the stares of everyone in the room. Kennedy grabbed her arm, anxiety blunting his brows, his mouth grim and purposeful.

She tried to peel his hand off her arm. "Let go of me."

"No. Hayley, for God's sake—"

"Get your hand off my arm."

The thought of another scene made her feel desperate. She pulled at his fingers, clawing and hurried. She had to get out of the restaurant, out of the hotel, out!

Kennedy clamped both hands on her upper arms, attempting to help her back to her chair. "Hayley, don't fight me. Listen to me! Claudia's just blowing smoke. You'd know that if you'd think about it logically!"

Everything was rearranging inside her, huge blocks of herself shifting and tumbling, creating an explosion of misery fed by her own guilt. She couldn't be with Kennedy. She'd known it from the start. How had she convinced herself otherwise?

"Please, Kennedy." Hayley's voice was colder than the November wind that flapped through the hotel's awnings. "Let me go."

Kennedy tried to get through to her with his eyes, but hers were unseeing. He slowly released her arms, slashing his name with repressed fury across the check before following her rigid form out of the restaurant.

"Don't make more of this than it is," he said through clenched jaws, stepping in front of her in the lobby.

"How could I?" Tears stood in her gray eyes but she was cloaked in a frightening numbness. "It can't be any worse than it is."

Kennedy allowed himself some ghoulishly murderous thoughts about Claudia Jeffries before saying calmly, "I don't blame you for being upset. She was monstrous. And her aim was deadly, love."

"I don't want to talk about it."

She shifted away but Kennedy was quicker. He forced himself in front of her, fury, and a terrible growing fear, licking through his veins. "Damn it, Hayley. You're feeding your own guilt about this! Claudia Jeffries just zeroed in on all your insecurities and now you're running with them."

Hayley could see the door to her escape. She moved to one side, but Kennedy suddenly blocked her path. She turned the other way, but he was there before her.

"Are you all right, ma'am?"

The concerned doorman made Hayley blink. He was regarding Kennedy warily. Kennedy glared at him, and the doorman automatically looked around himself for help.

"I'm fine," Hayley said, her thin voice less than convincing. She cleared her throat and tried again. "Fine."

The doorman walked away, but his attention was

focused on Kennedy with the suspicion of a policeman dogging a thief.

Kennedy swore in frustration. "Come upstairs to my suite for a few minutes," he told her, fighting to keep from dragging her to the elevator with him. God, she looked so forlorn and vulnerable! His throat throbbed with her pain. "Let's talk. Please, love. You need to. I need to."

"No." She shook her head in a slow-motion move that defeated Kennedy.

There was nothing he could do as she backed away from him, making a wide circle. She was too disturbed to reason with. A feeling of impotence washed over him as he watched her hurry to the door to the underground lot. He stood in motionless defeat as Hayley's hand connected with the door, her battered elegance painful to behold.

Hayley came to herself enough to glance back once, but Kennedy's gaunt face, his grim unhappiness, blurred her vision with a thousand unspent tears. She jerked hard on the heavy door and fled into the cool corridor, blanking her mind to the injustice she'd just laid on Kennedy's head.

She ran from the specter of Claudia's wrath. Ran from the scene of hope and love she'd just played with Kennedy. Ran from all the frustration and worry she'd had at work. Ran from every last mistake she'd ever made in her life.

But most of all, she ran from herself.

Chapter Nine

The look on Bernadette's face would have warned Hayley that something was wrong had she not known already.

"Your father wants to see you," the secretary told her, her eyes filled with an emotion that looked like sympathy.

Hayley felt a growing uneasiness. "Right away?"

"He's asked me twice if you've come in yet."

Hayley's heart sank. Still recovering from the events of the night before, she wasn't sure she was ready for what had to be more bad news. Sleep had been an impossibility, and she knew she looked as tired as she felt. With slow steps she made her way down the muted hallway to her father's office. Claudia Jeffries had undoubtedly complained.

Hayley's features were drawn tight. She regretted the way she'd handled that whole scene. Claudia had touched a very raw nerve—Hayley's suspect professionalism over Kennedy Taft—but that still didn't excuse her behavior. She'd overreacted, assuming guilt that wasn't hers. Rationally, she knew that she hadn't done anything wrong—her relationship with Kennedy had begun after the trial and had had nothing to do with business. But emotionally . . . well, she hated herself for naively thinking their affair couldn't affect her career. Now she shuddered, too aware of the damage Claudia could cause.

But it was more than that. Much more. The way Hayley had treated Kennedy was unforgivable. He'd been hurting too; she knew that now. But all she could think about at that disastrous moment was escape.

Hardly a worthy excuse, she thought, grimacing.

She ran a hand through the tousled tresses of her hair—there'd been no time for a chignon when she'd finally awakened. Sleep had caught up with her at dawn, but by then it had been too late. Feeling bleary-eyed, she'd rushed through the steps of getting ready. No matter what else was in the wind, she was determined not to be late to work again.

Hayley sighed and tapped on her father's door with trepidation. At his distracted "Come in," she twisted the knob and entered his office.

"Hayley."

Her father's unsmiling face said it all. She hadn't seen that look of stern disappointment since she was a child. The ache inside her was growing to unbelievable proportions. It had become a huge, yawning void that was threatening to swallow her up.

Jason Sinclair looked at the deep circles beneath his daughter's eyes. "Did you see "Portland Today" this morning?"

Hayley sank into a chair, the void inching wider. "Portland Today" was a local talk show, which featured news, gossip and several guest speakers each morning. "No," she said, premonition traveling up her spine.

"Claudia Jeffries was the featured guest."

"Oh, my God." Despair slumped her shoulders.

"I imagine you already know what she said."

Hayley met her father's gaze in wordless anguish. Oh, she knew all right. And now half the state of Oregon did too.

Her father eased himself into his chair, steepling his fingers, the corners of his mouth drawn downward. He sighed deeply. "She made some outrageous claims," he said unhappily. "The interviewer had to cut her off several times. I won't belabor all the gory details, but suffice it to say, Claudia Jeffries thinks you deliberately sabotaged her case."

Hayley made a small moan of protest.

"I don't have to tell you I know that's not true," her father went on. He frowned down at his hands. "You have too much integrity."

"Thank you." Hayley's voice was barely audible. She could scarcely believe this was happening.

"Luckily, "Portland Today's" host made a point of letting the audience know that Claudia Jeffries's claims had yet to be authenticated. However—" Hayley inwardly cringed at the harshness of her father's tone, the betrayal of his hidden anger "—she alluded to your relationship with Mr. Taft as being something more than professional. I was naturally outraged at that. I scoffed at her allegations. But Hayley, she cited an instance that was damn convincing."

Jason Sinclair never swore. Ever. Hayley felt a bottomless regret, a physical ache that made her sick with herself.

Her father heaved a deep sigh, looking all of his sixty-two years. "Did you have dinner with Kennedy Taft at the Cheswick last night?"

Were she in another frame of mind, she might have resented this intrusion into her personal life. But the situation had gone way too far to worry about protecting her privacy.

"Yes."

Her father looked grave. "Is your interest in him personal?"

Hayley's throat was dry. Oh, God. It was even worse than she'd imagined. "Yes."

It was Jason Sinclair's soft groan that undid her. It was packed with misery and disappointment. Something broke inside Hayley, some tiny hold on her self-respect. She desperately fought the urge to cry.

"What were you thinking of?" her father demanded. "My God, Hayley. It doesn't matter that you've done nothing legally wrong—the scandal will ruin your professional reputation!"

He rubbed a tired hand across his forehead, a

resigned, defeated move that made her die a little inside. "I'm sure you already know that you've tainted the image of Sinclair, Holmsby, and Layton along with it. Our business demands discretion, and a certain amount of personal scrutiny. What do you think our other clients will do?"

Hayley envisioned the panic this fiasco would create. Businessmen, alarmed by the notoriety that Hayley had brought to the case, would look elsewhere for representation. She was stabbed by a new, terrible fear. "Has anyone called you—about this?" she asked, her face growing whiter.

"It isn't the cavalcade it could be," her father assured her. "I've only had one call."

So far . . .

Hayley heard the unspoken words. Already one client had dropped them. She trembled at the realization that everything Sinclair, Holmsby, and Layton stood for could come tumbling down like a house of cards. The firm was built on professional integrity. Even though she was essentially guiltless, she'd let them all down.

She was sick with self-recrimination.

"Do you want me to quit?" she whispered.

"No, no." Her father waved that aside. "Let's not give up without a fight. It's bad, Hayley. I won't deceive you on that. But it's not irreparable. Claudia's just shrewish enough to antagonize people. There are probably a lot of people who saw that interview who won't believe a word of it."

But that isn't why one of our clients dropped us, is it?

Hayley's voice became stronger. "Is there something you want me to do? Some statement you'd like me to make?"

"Not at this time. Let Claudia Jeffries rave. . . ."

He didn't dismiss her, but Hayley sensed he'd finished what he wanted to say. He looked utterly deflated, and tears of self-disgust pricked her lids.

Her fingers were balled into tortured fists. She wanted to apologize but knew the words would sound as hollow as she felt inside.

"Hayley . . ."

She was rising from her chair; his tone stiffened her to attention.

"This Kennedy Taft. Is he worth it?"

It was a terribly unfair question for her father to ask her. But then, she'd been unfair to him, to the company he'd worked his whole life to establish.

"Yes."

Her answer neither pleased nor displeased him. He just regarded her through tired, thoughtful eyes.

As Hayley walked to the door, she heard him softly say, "I had a feeling he must be. . . ."

"Well?"

Matthew was planted in her office, looking more upset than even her father had.

"Well, what? I'm still employed." Hayley's disgust with herself spilled into her voice, as she added bitterly, "After all, I'm the boss's daughter. I get preferential treatment, you know. I can walk on water."

Matthew looked pained. "Don't, Hayley."

"Why not? It's what everyone thinks."

"It's what *you* think everyone thinks. Give us all a little more credit, huh?"

Hayley's martyred bravado failed. Her shoulders slumped. "Ah, let's face it, Matthew," she said wearily. "I blew it. I really blew it. Did you know one of our clients has already dropped us?"

Matthew tried to mask his surprise but he couldn't quite manage it before Hayley saw. "Which one?" he asked anxiously.

Even through her haze of self-disgust Hayley noticed he seemed unusually perturbed. "I don't know. But I'm sure we'll find out. God, I'm sorry."

"Hey—" Matthew managed an encouraging, if somewhat shaky, smile. "Don't be so hard on yourself. It'll all work out."

Hayley shook her head. "Now look who's comforting whom. The tables have turned."

Matthew's hand dropped in a friendly gesture on her shoulder. "Not for long," he assured her. "Things'll get better for you before you know it."

Hayley gave him a searching look. His hand was trembling. "I wish I had your confidence," she said slowly.

He patted her affectionately and drew away. "Well, if things don't get better for you, they're bound to get worse for me, so either way, you'll soon be the one offering comfort." He moved quickly to the door. "Hey, how about dinner tonight?" Then he frowned. "Or are you seeing . . . Taft . . . ?"

"No." Hayley squared her shoulders and walked to the back side of her desk. "That's over."

And the sad truth was, it truly was. She harbored no false hopes on that score. She'd treated him abominably. He would hardly stick around for more of the same.

But after Matt left, Hayley found herself unable to think about anything but Kennedy. What was he doing now? What was he thinking? Had he seen the show?

Hayley pinched the bridge of her nose, anguished by his image torturing her thoughts. He'd said he loved her, and she had a feeling that even after last night, he probably still did. He wasn't the type of man to stop loving so easily. Yet, he wasn't the type to take the kind of abuse she'd dished out either.

Locked in indecision, Hayley placed a hand across her mouth and stared at the phone. It was her move. With everything that had come down this morning, she hadn't considered the fact that Kennedy might still be willing to talk to her. She'd just figured it was over. *Finis.*

But it might not be, an eager voice inside her prompted.

Hayley yanked her desk drawer open and grabbed the phone book. After several tense moments she found the number of the Cheswick.

The line seemed to ring forever before a harried voice answered curtly.

Hayley drew in a courageous breath. "Hello, I'd like to speak to Mr. Kennedy Taft. I'm not certain which room he's in."

She counted the seconds while she was put on hold, then the desk clerk came back on.

"I'm sorry, miss. Mr. Taft checked out early this morning."

The airport was packed with travelers of every shape and size. Kennedy hoisted his canvas-and-leather garment bag over one shoulder and surveyed the melee with dark, angry eyes. Frustration was a poison that had infected his mood from the moment Hayley had run out on him. He couldn't wait to get out of the city.

Half a dozen times this morning he'd picked up the phone to call Hayley. He was concerned about her. She'd been in emotional shock the night before. How, he wondered, had she gotten through the morning?

But, with the receiver in hand, his sanity had invariably returned. She didn't want him around. *That* had been made patently clear. If ever she needed him, it was now, but she was too blasted stubborn, or independent, or prideful, to recognize it. All he wanted to do was cradle her to his chest and soothe some of her pain, but Hayley's rejection had been total. It didn't take a hell of a lot of insight to get the message.

"I've got a flight to Los Angeles," Kennedy said to the ticket agent. "Ten-thirty."

The keys of the computer made quick, hollow sounds, then the agent asked, "Smoking or non-smoking?"

"Whatever."

He stuffed the ticket into the inside pocket of his

jacket, glancing at his watch. A half hour until flight time. It felt like an eternity.

A once-in-a-lifetime thing . . .

Kennedy grimaced, walking toward the long concourse that led to his United Airlines flight. There was a line at the detection gate and he chafed at the delay. His words were coming back to mock him . . . to haunt him.

She'd said she loved him—though, he freely admitted, he'd practically forced her to. Still, Hayley wasn't the type of woman to say things just to please a man. She'd meant it.

Kennedy slung his garment bag onto the moving belt, walking through the metal-detection door without a hitch. He grabbed the bag and strode toward his departure gate.

A bank of empty telephone booths to his right seemed to beckon him. He tightened his grip around the handle of his bag and focused his gaze straight ahead, battling the urge to call with all of his not inconsiderable will.

But his mind was not so easily convinced.

Y-E-S . . . as in I love you . . .

"Damn."

With a sharp movement that made the plump woman behind him gasp in affront, Kennedy wheeled around, beelining toward the telephones. One more time. One last chance. What could it hurt? He'd given her everything he had to give already. Another rejection at this point was just more water under the bridge.

The receptionist at Sinclair, Holmsby, and Layton

rang Hayley's extension. Kennedy listened tensely, counting the rings with mounting uneasiness. Wasn't she at work? What had happened?

"Hayley Sinclair's office."

The male voice that answered made Kennedy feel wary. "Is Miss Sinclair there?" he asked cautiously.

"She can't come to the phone right now. Could I take a message?"

Kennedy suddenly recognized the voice. "Matthew Andrews?" he questioned quickly.

A pause followed. "Mr. Taft?"

Kennedy opted for straightforwardness. "I need to speak to Hayley right away. It's urgent." Matthew's hesitation made him impatient. "I've got a plane to catch any minute. Would you please put her on?"

"She's in a meeting."

Kennedy wondered if that was really true. Matthew's tone suggested it wasn't. Hanging on to his patience, he took the offensive. "Why are you in her office?"

Matthew made a surprised sound. "Well, I was just—down the hall . . . I—" He stopped and cleared his throat, angry at Kennedy's nerve. "I heard her phone ringing and decided to answer it," he answered stiffly.

"What kind of a meeting is she in?"

"I'd say it's one about you, Mr. Taft."

Kennedy gritted his teeth. He hadn't meant to antagonize Matthew but the lawyer's attitude had fanned his frustration. Unfortunately, Kennedy could feel waves of hostility coming across the line. He'd lost a potential ally.

Furious with himself for handling things all wrong, Kennedy said tersely, "I need to get a message to her." He could just imagine what kind of hell Hayley was going through.

"Sorry." Matthew Andrews didn't sound anything of the sort. "She doesn't want to speak to you. Her career's on the line, largely because of you."

"Is this your interpretation of how she feels?" Kennedy demanded angrily. "Or is it Hayley's?"

"Hayley's. I'll give her your message."

Matthew's curt tone wasn't lost on Kennedy. Whatever he hoped to say to Hayley was going to have to wait; Andrews would sabotage anything he tried to get across.

"Flight 217 ready for boarding."

Kennedy heard the disembodied voice and was swamped with renewed frustration. "Just tell her I'll call her," he said tersely, slamming down the phone.

His steps were swift and angry, propelled by his inner turmoil. He hated himself for what was happening to Hayley, blamed himself for jeopardizing her career. And now he felt as if he were running out on her, but the hell of it was—it was just what she wanted!

He was filled with a helpless feeling of impotence, and the curious notion that he was being set up in some way. Something just didn't seem to jibe right, but the whole crazy affair with Hayley had been that way. Maybe Gordon was right. Maybe he did need to get back to Hollywood and an entirely different perspective.

As he boarded the plane, he was assaulted by a

blast of cold Portland air. It knifed through him, a jolt of pain that had more to do with what he was losing than the condition of the weather.

"Damn it all to hell," he muttered, hearing the slam of metal against metal and a high-powered whine as the jet's door closed and its engines accelerated.

It was amazing, Hayley concluded, how normal life could become even after the most major upheaval. For the first few days after Claudia's appearance on "Portland Today," Hayley had been the topic on everyone's tongue at Sinclair, Holmsby, and Layton. She'd been a major news story too, but when nothing could be confirmed by her office, the press moved on to something else.

But Claudia Jeffries was out for blood. She'd wasted no time in meeting with the head of Sinclair, Holmsby, and Layton—Hayley's father—and had declared she was filing a misrepresentation suit against Hayley. Not a man to be ruffled easily, Jason Sinclair had told her to do whatever she felt she needed to do, and Claudia had left in a huff.

During those hours, and days, and weeks that followed, Hayley lived in a state of mild anxiety, part numbness, part pure disbelief. Her meeting with Warren Smythe was postponed and rescheduled, owing to Claudia's allegations, and by the time the day finally arrived, Hayley was in a much calmer state of mind.

Warren didn't waste time. "Claudia wants to sue you," he said distinctly, as soon as they were closeted in the conference room. "I told her not to."

Hayley blinked, astonished. She could only stare at the other attorney, waiting.

"I'm here to discuss the Taft trial, that's all, Hayley." He smiled faintly. "If I thought I could make any money by representing Claudia against you, I'd do it. But, unfortunately, that's not the case. We'd lose."

"Unfortunate for whom?" Hayley asked dryly, too relieved to be angered by Warren's avarice.

Warren just shrugged. "The Taft case is a different story. I think I can win the appeal. Now, let's get to it. . . ."

Hayley had answered all Warren's questions and tried to be polite, if not entirely helpful. Inside, her heart was still bleeding. Each mention of Kennedy's name brought another splinter of pain.

Warren's interview had forced Hayley to think about Kennedy, something she'd steadfastly refused to do. Matthew had told her that Kennedy had called, but something in his face—a kind of distant anger—had warned her that whatever Kennedy had said wouldn't be something she wanted to hear. Matthew's vagueness had kept her from delving too deeply; she could vividly imagine the kind of uneasy, pat excuses Kennedy had given for leaving.

Kennedy had called her a second time, after his plane had landed in California, and that time he'd connected with her.

"Hayley. Are you all right?"

His low, anxious voice had been a caress to her senses, yet a jarring pain too. With resignation she'd realized the old axiom had come true: She couldn't live with him, yet she couldn't live without him.

"I'm fine," she had lied.

"I called you earlier."

"I know. Matthew told me."

Hayley could hear the noises of the Los Angeles airport behind him, could feel the distance between them. It had made her loneliness an acute, throbbing despair, one that might lessen with time but would never truly disappear.

"Don't believe that frustrated, mercenary bitch," Kennedy had warned fiercely. "Don't let her hurt you."

Hayley had had to wait for the tears that burned her eyes to relent before she could answer. "I'm okay," she'd managed. "Last night, I just felt everything coming down. Really, I'm fine."

Except I'm dying for you, Kennedy.

"Do you need me to come back?"

His voice was so expressionless that Hayley hadn't been able to read what he really felt. She'd wondered, *If I asked, would he turn around and catch the next flight to Portland?* She had ached to know, but been unable to make such a selfish demand.

Instead, she'd forced determination to her voice. "No," she'd said, dredging up the remains of her self-respect, letting him go. "Let's not make more of this than there is."

Silence had hummed across the wire, unspoken dreams, unfulfilled desires. "I'll call you," he had promised.

"Yes. Do that."

That had been the end, and Hayley had refused to think about it since. She'd hung up the phone, locked the door to her office, then cried in noiseless misery at what she'd lost. Huge, silent tears had slipped down her cheeks and she'd just let them run, pouring out her soul. It was a rare indulgement but one she'd felt deserving of. In her mind, it had been a purge, a way to wipe the slate clean and start again.

In her heart, however, it hadn't worked out quite that way. After the meeting with Warren, she had had to face that fact and try to push Kennedy to her peripheral thoughts. He was a past chapter, so it was time to forget him.

It almost worked, too.

For Hayley, days melded together, one so like another that she seldom noticed the date. Her life became narrowed into a succession of appointments and hearings, none of which were particularly earth-shattering since the beating her reputation had taken after the Taft fiasco.

It was her nights that were the worst. She had too much time to think about herself. Although her career was still functioning, she wasn't. And forgetting Kennedy was turning into a full-time occupation. Without him she was an emotional zombie. Matthew tried to pull her out of her slump, but Hayley just couldn't quite manage it. Even her father had expressed concern over her lifelessness.

"If you need a vacation, Hayley, take it," he'd urged. "Once you let depression in, it can take over your life. I mean it. No one's worth it."

It had struck her much, much later that he'd zeroed in on Kennedy as being the cause, not the controversy surrounding Claudia Jeffries and the trial. Making a conscious effort to perk up hadn't been easy for her—it still wasn't—but Hayley had finally tamed her emotions into submission. If she had to live a lonelier life than before, so be it. She'd made the decision about loving Kennedy, fully aware of the price.

As a way to keep from dwelling on past mistakes, Hayley focused all her attention on the Tom Wilson reverse-discrimination suit. The trial date had been set for early March, and when not consumed by the day-to-day pressures that came up each work day, she spent her time carefully preparing her case. The Wilson suit could be, she sensed, an excellent opportunity for her, a way to restore her credibility and reputation. And so far—she crossed her fingers superstitiously—Tom Wilson hadn't passed her over for someone with a less notorious reputation.

The reverse-discrimination suit was all she had though, and Hayley, feeling battleworn and wary of believing in bright, shining futures that didn't really exist, let each day pass with no real enthusiasm for what would be. Without Kennedy, it didn't seem to matter a whole lot anyway.

Chapter Ten

*K*ennedy stared at the fir-beamed ceiling of his beach-front home and wondered if he would lose the tattered remains of his sanity altogether. His patience was already gone, and his reputation for being a man with a coolly rational mind and approach was taking a beating. One more minor calamity and he was going to lose it altogether with the whole damn picture.

"Look, Carrie. That's an editing problem," he said to his latest source of irritation. "Shooting's over. You'll have to lodge your complaint with Titan, not me."

"But I thought you'd help me. I thought you liked me, Kennedy." Carrie moaned softly, her fear of dealing with the film studio evident.

Kennedy fiercely pinched the bridge of his nose,

knowing his impatience with her now was partly to blame for the poor girl's insecurity. But it wasn't totally. She was gorgeous and ingenuous, and bound to be the biggest sex symbol since Bo Derek, but she just couldn't act. And she knew it.

Inwardly sighing, Kennedy realized he'd shown more kindness to her during the production than some of the more seasoned actors and actresses, and now it was coming back to haunt him. But he was only guilty of feeling sorry for her; his interest in her ended there. She'd been overwhelmed by the fame of her costars—something that hadn't helped her performance—and Kennedy had tried to ease her feelings of inadequacy all through filming.

Luckily, he was through with *Pleasure Hunt*. Directing it, anyway. Personally, he thought it was a rather trashy flick, but that probably wouldn't affect box office receipts. It had enough glitz, action, romance and comedy to appeal to a wide range of viewers. The critics would probably crucify it, but Kennedy had long ago given up worrying about what they thought.

"Talk to Gordon Woodrow," Kennedy said, trying to soothe the anxious star-to-be. "The picture hasn't been final-edited yet and if you're really worried about the Monaco scene with Trent, tell him. He'll listen."

And then tell you the same thing he has for the last month: the casino scene with Trent Wickson stays in.

"You really think he will?" Carrie asked dubiously, hopefully.

"He'll listen. That's the only guarantee I can give."

A huge sigh filled Kennedy's ear. "Okay, I'll try. At least I can trust you."

Kennedy winced as he hung up the phone. She was going to have to learn about misplaced trust somewhere along the line; her naiveté was going to get her into trouble. He felt a fleeting regret as he pondered what would become of her, though he supposed she'd make out all right.

She certainly found a way to stir up your sympathies, he thought in self-mockery.

Kennedy scowled, considered pouring himself a drink, then decided on a walk onto his back deck instead. He stood with his hands in his back pockets, the sea breeze damp against his face. Waves ruffled on the sand, startlingly white in contrast to the horizonless darkness of night sky and sea.

He knew, without having to depend on Gordon's pop psychology, that his interest in Carrie—though nothing more than friendship—had been piqued by a pair of wide, soulful gray eyes. Those eyes, and her ingenuity, had forced unwelcome memories of Hayley into Kennedy's mind.

He'd been trying hard to forget her; the futility in loving her had been obvious after their last conversation. But Carrie's facial resemblance to Hayley had made it all but impossible. Kennedy had found himself using his own free time to get her over the rough spots, dredging up extra patience coaching her, spending more hours with her than her newcomer status deserved and inadvertently raising a few eyebrows in the process.

But Kennedy had put Carrie through her paces,

eking a credible performance from her—something he freely admitted had a lot to do with his own talent. Whatever whispers had started on location had been quashed by Kennedy's insistence that Carrie do it right, his strictness and professionalism during the filming of her scenes. The trouble was, now he had his own starry-eyed fan. Carrie was smart enough to know what he'd done for her, and smarter still to realize that generally there was a future price to pay. And she was happily eager to come up with any payment Kennedy might demand. . . .

Only he wasn't interested.

Kennedy sighed, his thoughts as dark as the starless sky. The only one who truly understood what was in his head was Gordon, and he'd just regarded him dolefully, with that mock hangdog expression that crossed his face every time Kennedy turned down another available "torso."

"Wake up, pal. Life is too short to be so selective," Gordon had cautioned.

"And it's way too long to pile up a bunch of mistakes that you have to wade through when you're old," Kennedy had rejoined.

"Bad philosophy, man." Gordon's scowl epitomized his fear of aging.

"Yeah? Well, don't say anything that'll make me spout it, then."

Now Kennedy wondered if he hadn't been a little hasty. Oh, he wasn't interested in Carrie. God forbid. But, even with the way everything had happened, he was sorry he'd given up on Hayley. She'd been worth more effort; of that he was painfully certain.

It was too late now, however. Too much time had passed.

Kennedy rubbed his chin. If he was completely honest with himself, he might even admit that he'd been a trifle scared of the commitment that had been traveling toward him at the speed of a freight train. He'd fallen in love so quickly. The pace had been staggering! And then Hayley's rejection . . .

He inhaled sharply. *Had that just been a convenient excuse?*

Kennedy swore softly, wheeling back to the living room, deciding a drink was just the ticket after all. He sloshed some liquid into a glass, tiny lines pinched between his brows in intense introspection.

No. It hadn't been an excuse. He'd been willing to take the risk; it had been Hayley who hadn't. Maybe it had been a way to buy time, however; a delay of the inevitable, a chance to think things through. He'd used the production of *Pleasure Hunt* as a way to slow down the furious pace of his emotions.

But now *Pleasure Hunt* was over. At least his part in it. And he was no closer to getting over Hayley than he'd been the day he'd left Portland.

It was too late to call her tonight, he told himself, but his hand was already reaching for the receiver. Too little, too late, he warned himself. Too much time spent trying to patch things up over the telephone.

Two rings, three. It was interminable, a long-distance connection that seemed incredibly fragile across the miles.

"Hello?" Her voice sounded wide awake, and full of the innate caution a midnight call aroused.

"Hello, Hayley." Kennedy's drawl was tight with expected rejection. He rubbed a weary hand across his face. "I would have waited to call you in the morning, but I couldn't think of a single reason to. I thought now might be better. Tell me if I'm wrong."

Her swift intake of breath was strangely reassuring. She was still affected by him, at least in some way. "Kennedy?" she asked.

"I'm here, love. Right here."

"Where?"

He realized she thought he was still working on *Pleasure Hunt*. His confidence growing, he said, "At home. Los Angeles. Southern California. I want you to come and join me."

The silence accused him, and he railed himself for moving too fast, too strong. He waited, expecting the worst—expecting her just to hang up.

But her voice was surprisingly light when she said, "I couldn't just pack up and leave."

He scarcely believed the words she'd spoken. Treading more carefully, he asked, "Does that mean you might like to?"

He could hear her silent, tortured indecision, before she whispered, "It means, why didn't you call me sooner?"

Kennedy's melancholy disappeared in a soaring rush. "You don't ask much, do you, Miss Sinclair? I distinctly remember getting the proverbial brush-off. Our last telephone conversation hurt."

"I'm sorry. I'm so sorry."

The inadequacy of her words sounded to him like a verbal wringing of her hands. He wished he could touch her, soothe her. "We're both sorry. If I could undo what's been done . . ."

This time her silence was thoughtful. "Things are better now, Kennedy. Claudia never followed through. She couldn't."

"I know." Of course he knew. If Claudia had really tried to sue Hayley, Kennedy would have made certain she regretted it to her dying day.

"She's still trying to appeal, though," Hayley went on, sounding desperate for conversation. "Warren Smythe—her new attorney—thinks they've got a case."

"That's not our problem."

"It's yours," Hayley argued. "And it feels like it's mine too."

He wanted to kiss her for that. "I love you," he said, the words tumbling out before he could get a rein on his sanity.

The small sound she made was one of . . . what? Distress? Relief? Joy? Kennedy closed his eyes and wished he could seem suave and uncaring when it really counted, when everything he wanted—needed —was on the line.

"I have to be in court on Monday," she said softly. "But . . ."

Her decision hung between them, waiting for him to grab it. Kennedy uttered a mute prayer of thanks, and said with rising jubilance, "Catch the earliest flight down tomorrow morning and we've got practically the whole weekend left."

"There's one that leaves around seven."

He smiled at her careful tone, understanding her

fears implicitly. "You'll be here by nine. I'll be at the airport, waiting."

"I don't know which flight it is—"

"It doesn't matter. There aren't that many from Portland. I'll find you, love. Never fear."

"Kennedy?"

"Yes?"

He heard a pain-filled hesitation and worried afresh that she would change her mind.

"I'll see you tomorrow," she said softly, then hung up before he could answer.

The keys to his Porsche were in Kennedy's hands when the doorbell chimed at eight o'clock the next morning. Determined to get rid of the intruder as quickly as possible, he grabbed his jacket and headed for the door, a little surprised that anyone he knew would be out and about so early on a Saturday.

"Gordon." Kennedy looked at Titan's production head with a mixture of annoyance and disbelief.

"I've got an appointment downtown," Gordon explained with grim impatience, "or else I'd never be here at this god-awful hour. Are you leaving?" Surprise lifted his brows.

Kennedy belatedly remembered he'd told Gordon he planned to be home all day. "Brooding," Gordon had accused, and Kennedy hadn't even bothered offering a return comment.

"I'm going to the airport," he explained to Gordon, glancing at the clock.

A grin crossed Gordon Woodrow's lean face.

"What? An unscheduled trip? Since when did you become so spur-of-the-moment?"

"I'm not going anywhere." Kennedy could see where the conversation was heading but was unable to deflect it. "I'm meeting someone," he said levelly.

Gordon didn't miss Kennedy's hostile tone. His face sobered as he said, "I suppose it's too much to hope that you're meeting someone other than Hayley Sinclair."

Kennedy had grown exceedingly tired of having to explain himself to Gordon Woodrow. He scowled. "Give it a rest, Gordon. Yes, it's Hayley." He met Gordon's gaze and reminded him in a low tone, "A lot of time's gone by since the trial."

Gordon sighed. "Not near enough, I'm afraid."

Kennedy ignored his cryptic remark. "Was there some specific reason you stopped by?"

Gordon hesitated, as if he had a lot more he wanted to say. Kennedy's unwavering stare made him clear his throat. "We really liked *Pleasure Hunt's* rough cut," he said, rubbing his hands distractedly. "It was great."

"But?"

"But nothing. The final editing's almost complete. I came by to offer congratulations, and to invite you to the viewing tomorrow night." He let his breath whoosh out in a heavy sigh. "Kennedy, I've got to talk to you."

Kennedy's eyes narrowed. "Be careful, Gordon. Advice on my personal life I don't need."

"That's where you're wrong."

Gordon's face became grimly serious, and Kennedy's annoyance grew into something else. A vague uneasiness centered in the pit of his stomach.

"The farther you stay away from Hayley Sinclair, the better," Gordon said suddenly, walking past Kennedy to the kitchen doorway.

Kennedy shut the front door, leaning his shoulder wearily against the jamb. He sensed that what was coming was something he wasn't going to want to hear. He also sensed that he needed to know.

He followed Gordon to the kitchen, where the grave-faced executive was pouring himself a cup of coffee.

Kennedy waited until their eyes met. "Why?"

His terseness wasn't lost on Gordon. Knowing Kennedy's sensitivity when it came to Hayley, he went straight to the point. "There's something rotten in her firm, Kennedy. Somebody's on the take."

"What do you mean?" Every muscle in Kennedy's face froze in unwelcome anticipation.

"Her firm offered to keep us abreast of their progress during your trial." Gordon's mouth twisted. "For a fee, that is. A large fee. A less scrupulous company than Titan could have known Hayley Sinclair's every move and stacked the deck against Claudia Jeffries."

Kennedy was shocked to silence. Seconds passed, then, harshly, he exclaimed, "I don't believe it."

"Believe it, friend. It's the truth."

"Who made the offer?" Kennedy's hand balled into a fierce fist.

Gordon made a sound of unhappiness, his lips

turning downward. Kennedy's stomach knotted, rejection stiffening his spine as he fully understood. "It's not Hayley," he said instantly.

"Kennedy—"

"It's not." His hand clenched and unclenched, heart thudding. "Tell me it's not, Gordon," he said in a taut whisper.

"I wish I could," Gordon said, meaning it. "I really wish I could, but the fact is, we don't know who's behind it. The offer was sent by letter, a typewritten message on Sinclair, Holmsby, and Layton's printed letterhead. But it was very specific."

"It could have been a hoax," Kennedy argued.

Gordon nodded. "It could have been." He eyed his friend, genuinely wishing he hadn't had to be the one to tell him. "What do *you* think?" he asked.

Kennedy was suffering a deep and bitter anguish. He finally grasped the significance of Gordon's aversion to Hayley—and he wished he didn't. He told himself he didn't believe she was the culprit; she had too much integrity, too much honor. Yet when he thought about the whole series of events objectively, logically, it was easy to see how he could have been duped.

But it would have taken a very clever actress to pull it off. Hayley was no actress.

"What did Titan do, after the offer was received?" Kennedy asked thinly.

"Nothing." Gordon shrugged. "We were supposed to respond to a post office address within ten days of receipt of the letter. We just let the deadline expire."

"And that was that?" Kennedy's green eyes stared at him.

Gordon lifted his palm. "We decided to wait and see the outcome of your trial."

Kennedy's numbed senses began to function. "And if I'd lost . . . ?"

Gordon bowed his head in guilty acquiescence. "Then you could have declared a mistrial. Titan would have backed you all the way."

"Nice of you to tell me!" Kennedy's fist slammed down on the counter next to Gordon, causing the empty coffee mug to topple onto its side, swinging in a narrow accusing arc between the two men. "Damn it, Gordon! Why didn't you let me know?"

"Because you won," he said simply. "And you'll win the appeal too."

Kennedy dropped into one of the taupe canvas armchairs, his head falling back against the cushions, eyes closed. "You calculating bastard," he said without heat.

"Yeah? Well, save your swearing for Miss Sinclair's law firm. Somebody there is sweetening her own pockets."

"Her?"

"Just a guess," Gordon hastened to put in, seeing the swift change in Kennedy's expression. "But I'd bet money on Hayley Sinclair. For God's sake, Kennedy," he exploded, seeing anger darken the other man's face, "she's the logical choice. Look how she gained your confidence! Who else would take that kind of risk? She had to be pretty sure of herself."

Kennedy's blood was boiling, yet suspicions were

darting across his mind, suspicions he desperately wanted to kill. It wasn't Hayley. It couldn't be. But if what Gordon said was true—and Kennedy knew he wouldn't lie—then whom did that leave, but Hayley?

Kennedy's chest hurt. An ache was spreading through his muscles, paralyzing him. He had firsthand knowledge of what lengths women could go to meet their own ends. His ex-wife had been an excellent teacher.

"It's someone else," Kennedy said, raking despairing fingers through his hair.

Gordon didn't answer. He fished in his pocket for a cigarette, then remembered that he'd quit. He sighed deeply. After a moment he asked quietly, "Who?"

Kennedy's jaw tightened. "Hayley's not capable of it," he said, determined in her defense. "Especially not for money."

Out of the blue, a scene passed through his mind: He and Hayley seated across from each other at the Den. A quiet, sensual intimacy stretching between them. Dim lights, soft, blurring voices, and Hayley saying, "I'm not totally selfless, Mr. Taft."

His fingers shook as he pressed them to his temples. *She could have been laughing at you.*

"Well, what are you going to do about her?"

Kennedy opened his eyes to see Gordon's unsmiling face. He sat in silence for a long time, the antique clock on the wall ticking the passing seconds with quiet authority.

"I'm going to pick her up at the airport," he said, pushing himself upward with his palms.

"And then?"

"And then I'm going to ask her what the hell's going on at Sinclair, Holmsby, and Layton."

"Be careful. You've got an appeal hanging in the wings."

Kennedy swore once, pungently. "That's hardly my biggest concern at this point."

"Listen, Kennedy. Titan hasn't gone to trial yet; in fact we're trying not to. We're planning to settle with Claudia and possibly kill your appeal at the same time."

"Do that." Kennedy was heading for the door.

"What I'm telling you," Gordon yelled, his voice rising in irritation at Kennedy's total disregard for trying to save his own, and Titan Pictures', neck, "is not to rock the boat. That little nine-year-old girl. Lisa Jeffries? You do remember her, don't you?"

Kennedy stopped and turned, waiting. "Yes."

"Well, you're going to get your wish, pal. Titan's offered Claudia a bundle, and half is tied in trust for Lisa."

"Has Claudia accepted?"

"Not yet, but all signs are positive."

Kennedy tried to feel good about the news but his chest was still in a stranglehold of betrayal. "How come you're not going to trial?" he asked, as they went outside together.

Gordon snorted. "You may have won, but we probably wouldn't. No jury looks at a company being sued the same way they do an individual. It would cost us five times more to go to trial and lose."

Kennedy watched Gordon roar off in his copper-colored Mercedes, his thoughts grim. He was late to meet Hayley already, but some things couldn't be rushed. He needed time to clear his head. He needed time to assure himself that Hayley wouldn't use him in the way Gordon had suggested. He didn't believe she would. He didn't believe he could let himself get tricked by an unscrupulous female again.

Yet . . .

Dying a little inside, Kennedy walked toward his car. The jubilation that had been building since his call to Hayley the night before had soured. Now he felt wretched. And the worst of it was he still loved her. Guilt or innocence wasn't even an issue.

He still loved Hayley Sinclair.

Chapter Eleven

*H*ayley collected her overnight bag from the slowly circling baggage carousel, her gray eyes anxiously searching the crowd. She hadn't doubted Kennedy's ability to find her last night, but now she wished she'd been a little more specific about carriers and times.

She shook her head at the baggage claim valet and hoisted the leather strap over one shoulder, looking around her. The arrival crowds were thick, even at this hour in the morning, and the whole scene was one of pandemonium.

Hayley squeezed her way through the milling throng, smiling to herself as she remembered one comic's wry assessment of the huge international airport: "You've got to worry about a city with an airport named LAX."

Well, it was hardly lax today. Los Angeles International was currently a hub of frenzied activity—people and parcels and airport personnel all jumbled together. Hayley was a bit overwhelmed by the sheer size of it all, and she guiltily reminded herself how wrong she'd been in believing all that "laid-back" Southern California propaganda. Kennedy had told her she was a reverse snob. Maybe she had been, at that.

Kennedy. The thought of seeing him again brought a quick thrill of excitement. He didn't know it yet, but she'd been on the verge of calling him before he beat her to the punch. It was as if the timing were suddenly right; they couldn't be victimized by it now.

The past few months had given her ample time to think. Maybe too much time; she'd worried the smallest memories of those passionate few days with Kennedy to death. She'd even tried to analyze her feelings away, but it had been a useless endeavor: she loved him as much now as she had then.

She even wondered why she'd allowed the split to happen at all. She loved him. He loved her. With that base, how could any other problem be insurmountable?

Her mouth quirked wryly. So simple really. Yet for a wild few days she'd felt everything coming down on her, so much so that she hadn't been able to distinguish what really mattered. Thank God she'd finally gotten her perspective back!

Hayley was about to ask directions to a phone when she saw Kennedy walking through the automatic glass doors from the outside street. A backdrop of noise, traffic and sunny skies followed him inside, but Hayley was mesmerized by the man himself—a memory come to shocking life. Lean and muscled, slim-hipped, with a confident walk and commanding presence, Kennedy Taft hit Hayley's emotions with the same unconscious power that had bowled her over in the courtroom.

He wore faded jeans and an open-throated forest green shirt, a far cry from the serious, impeccably dressed man she'd met in Portland. Yet clothes were hardly the issue. There was something about him that took her breath away.

He brushed back a breeze-scattered lock of hair, and scanned the room. When his eyes fell on Hayley she lifted a hand in greeting, her smile faltering slightly at something in his face—a grave hardness that didn't seem to disappear when he recognized her.

He doesn't want me here!

Hayley's stomach dropped, her heart suddenly pounding with misery. *He's reconsidered, and he doesn't want me after all.*

He stopped several feet in front of her, surveying her with intent silvery green eyes that froze her where she stood. Hayley's lips parted in mute protest, her eyes locked to his.

His face altered slightly. "God, I've missed you," he said feelingly.

"Oh, Kennedy . . ."

Relief slumped her shoulders and he reached for her bag at the same instant, the strap sliding neatly into his palm.

It was going to be all right, she thought thankfully. Everything was going to be all right.

"You don't know how glad I am to hear those

words," she murmured, her smile growing more secure.

"Why?" His hand touched her back, guiding her toward the glass doors that led outside. "I thought we cleared all that up last night."

"I thought we did too," Hayley admitted. "But when I saw you . . ." She lifted her shoulders dismissively, lips curving gently. "Paranoia runs deep, I guess."

Hayley saw a line form between his brows, but the next second it was gone. Once again, her overactive senses picked up bad vibes, and she inwardly scolded herself for her ridiculous fears. Still, she couldn't help asking, "Is something wrong?"

Kennedy unlocked the door to his car, helping her inside before he answered. "The only thing wrong," he assured her, "is that we've wasted too much time already. And I intend to take care of that, starting now. . . ."

Hayley relaxed against the leather cushions; Kennedy's scent, seductive and masculine, filled the warm interior of the car. His words were full of hunger, and she tried to be relieved. Still, uneasiness seemed crouched just below her skin, making perspiration gather between her breasts. She wondered why she was picking up mixed messages.

Kennedy drove like a native through the multilane traffic. Hayley had to admire his nerve; she was certain she would have let other drivers push her aside.

"I can't believe I'm really here," she murmured, looking out the window at the morning brightness.

The sky was high and blue, with only a hint of the gray smog that collected in the inner basin.

"Neither can I. After all—" he stretched out an encompassing palm "—this is L.A."

His grin turned her worries to dust. Hayley's spirits climbed at his gentle mockery.

"Metropolitan heart of the decadent West," she rejoined. "I may never be the same."

"Mmmm." The tiny crow's-feet beside his eyes bunched in humor. "Have you ever been here before?"

"Once. I was six years old. I try to vacation in less populated areas."

Hayley let herself enjoy watching him as he drove. She'd been silly to be so uptight. Silly and paranoid. The only thing wrong between them was the amount of time they'd wasted while being apart. She loved him, and at the first opportunity, she intended to tell him so. He'd already leaped over that hurdle the night before.

Kennedy caught her watching him. "Then I think you need a little street advice," he said.

"Street advice?"

He nodded. "A speech I give to all my out-of-town guests."

Hayley was still mulling over what kind of out-of-town guests he might have when he began to lecture.

Adopting a grave air, he said, "First of all, don't talk to anyone, don't even look at them. In fact, don't even get out of your car. You won't need to anyway; there are more drive-in windows in Southern California than the sum total of the rest of the world. They're mandated by state law here.

"If you have to get out, be sure you have a good reason. Plain walking just doesn't cut it. You've got to jog. Bike riding's accepted as long as you wear the right apparel—biking shorts are a must."

Hayley's mouth was curved into a smile of unexpected surprise. She was divided between the desire to laugh out loud or throw her arms around him in a hug.

"But," Kennedy went on, slanting her a mocking look, "if you're really desperate for fresh air, go somewhere else. The smog'll kill you."

How could she have ever been apart from him? Hayley was consumed with loving him, and in that loving, knew she would do everything in her power to make it work between them.

"Sounds to me like a wonderful place to live," she murmured.

Kennedy's grin slowly waned, to be replaced by a curiously sober, almost bittersweet, expression. Hayley wondered what she'd said to cause the change; she felt the lightheartedness between them slipping away.

"It's not so bad," he said at length. "But it's not your kind of lifestyle, is it?"

Suddenly one of their biggest problems loomed between them. Hayley wished she could tell him the truth—that she didn't feel the disdain for his profession he'd once accused her of. But no words seemed totally adequate, so she answered his question as it stood.

"I don't know. I haven't spent much time out of Oregon." Calling on her courage, she inquired, "Does it matter so much to you, what I think?"

"I live here, Hayley." Kennedy's eyes were focused on the highway. "I'm not going to move. I couldn't, even if I wanted to."

"Because of your work."

It was a statement, not a question. Hayley understood only too well that Kennedy's job made it nearly impossible for him to live anywhere other than Hollywood or New York; he had to be at the center of his industry.

But did he honestly think she would ask him to give up his entire career for her? Or even put it on the back burner, for that matter?

It was reassuring, however, to know he was thinking along those lines.

Kennedy's eyes narrowed thoughtfully. "What about you, Hayley? What are you trying to accomplish in your career?" His mouth tightened, as he added, "Besides setting precedents, that is."

Once again Hayley was swept by that same feeling of uneasiness. It almost felt like he was interrogating her. "I don't know, really. I suppose I'd like to be a full partner in a law firm someday."

"Your father's?" Kennedy asked quickly.

She shook her head. "Possibly. I wouldn't even mind striking out on my own, but now's not the right time."

"When will be the right time?"

Hayley smoothed the line of her dress. "Hard to say," she answered slowly. "My reputation's taken a bit of a beating lately. I need some time to reestablish. Maybe if I could get some money together . . ." She trailed off, sensing a peculiar tightening of Kennedy's muscle and flesh.

A long moment passed. Hayley glanced at his chiseled profile, trying to guess what was circling his mind.

"What are you trying to say?" she asked at length. She laughed a trifle awkwardly, "I mean—this conversation . . ." Her hand fluttered helplessly. "Shouldn't it wait until we've had a chance to get reacquainted?"

He turned off onto a side street, the road winding to the north of Santa Monica, catching for a moment a brilliant view of ocean and sky meeting the sickled section of beach between Malibu and Redondo Beach.

"You're right." Kennedy's grip on the steering wheel seemed to loosen with an effort. He drew a long breath and let it out on a deep sigh.

Hayley had the feeling there was a lot he had deliberately left unsaid. But she pushed those thoughts angrily aside. She was furious with herself for becoming so paranoid. It—*he*—just mattered so much to her!

Kennedy's house was fronted by a stucco fence with a wrought-iron gate. Inside the drive, lush greenery and two immense palms covered the grounds that led to the terra cotta tiled entryway.

Hayley followed Kennedy through the front door, her admiration growing by leaps and bounds. The house was bathed in light from floor-to-ceiling win-

dows that covered the entire length of the back wall.
The ocean was several stories down, but the view
stretched for miles. Hayley could see tiny white flecks
on the water, which, upon closer inspection, turned
out to be sailboats and small cruisers. The whole
scene was such a far cry from the gloomy March skies
she'd just left that she was awed by its beauty.

"Your view is dazzling," she said, knowing even
that was an understatement.

Kennedy glanced up. "Yes," he said, after a moment's thought.

"You never told me it was this beautiful here."
Hayley smiled in self-mockery, waiting for him to
remind her of her prejudices about the area.

But Kennedy just smiled distractedly. "It never
came up. Want some coffee?"

He walked behind the kitchen bar and began going
through the motions before she could answer. Hayley
looked down at her bag, sitting forlornly in the middle
of the room where Kennedy had dropped it. She felt a
little like that—abandoned—and was bewildered by
Kennedy's strange attitude. He seemed to want her
one minute, disregard her the next.

"How was it, filming *Pleasure Hunt*?" she asked
when he gingerly placed the hot cup between her
palms.

"It had its ups and downs. Carrie Criswald—have
you heard of her?" At Hayley's blank look, Kennedy
swiftly went on, "She's a new actress—an unknown
whose face, and body," he admitted with a dry,
engaging smile, "will probably make her famous. It

won't be her talent, unfortunately, but then . . ." He frowned, wondering why he was telling Hayley about Carrie.

Hayley was perfectly still, her quietness saying she was going to wait until she'd heard why he was bringing up this young actress before making a move.

"Oh, hell . . ." Kennedy sighed. His mouth drooped unhappily. He loved her. It didn't matter what she'd done. *And he didn't believe she'd done anything! She couldn't have!*

"Are you trying to tell me something?" Hayley asked quietly. Her face had grown pale.

Kennedy set down his cup, hating himself for believing Gordon's theories. His callousness had already wounded her, and now he walked toward her quickly, conscious only of the need to wipe the look of expected doom from her face.

"Yes." His voice was harsh with the truth. "I am. I'm trying to tell you that Carrie Criswald has fantastic gray eyes that wouldn't let me forget you. I wanted to. God, did I want to. But I couldn't."

Hayley didn't dare believe what he was saying. Her emotions had already run the gamut from despair to jubilance and back again to despair. Words were nothing. Something was definitely wrong.

"It was that important to forget me?" she managed to force out.

Kennedy made a sound of disbelief. "It was you who forced me to make that decision. *You.* I didn't want to leave you. You wanted me to leave."

Hayley bowed her head. Her cup trembled in her

hands. "That was a mistake. Just one more in a succession of many," she said with a trace of bitterness.

Kennedy stopped instantly. "Most mistakes can be rectified quite easily," he said.

Again she felt that warning, as if there were more things unspoken than said. She couldn't understand it.

"Kennedy . . . I get the feeling . . ."

"What?"

Hayley shook her head. "I wish I knew," she murmured. He was close enough to her to feel the heat from his skin. It occurred to her at that moment that he hadn't really tried to touch her once. It was as if he was deliberately holding himself back.

Hayley set her untouched cup on a glass end table, hiding her anxieties. She'd come prepared to pour out her feelings, letting him know how much she loved him. Now she felt off-balance, as if the ground between them had become slippery and loaded with hidden mines.

She managed a shaky laugh, her honey blond hair swinging in bafflement around her head. "Is there something you're not telling me? If there is, I'd prefer you'd just come out with it." Hayley pressed her hands together, concentrating on honesty. "I get the distinct feeling that something's not quite right. As if there's some hang-up between us now that wasn't there before."

Kennedy looked at her for a long moment. He sighed, making Hayley's pulse jump. She was right. There was something!

"Tell me, Kennedy." Her voice trembled slightly.

His mouth was a thin line. "There's nothing wrong."

Hayley's heart flipped over in pain. He was lying; she knew it. "Something's bothering you."

"No."

"Is it me? Do you want me to leave?"

"No!"

"Then what?"

Tremors of fear were running beneath her skin when Kennedy's arms were suddenly thrown around her, a crushing, heavenly embrace. Hayley went weak, her emotions wrung out. She buried her face in the comfort of his shoulder, glad for the real security of flesh and bone. His words were scaring her.

"I love you," she confessed, gambling with the only thing she had to offer.

"Oh, Hayley . . ."

Kennedy's chin was against her hair, his voice thick with emotion.

"If that's too honest—too soon to tell you—"

"No." He lifted her chin up, desire and love and something else dangerously mixed in the silver highlights of his eyes. "No, no, love. Nothing's too soon. . . ."

"I was never good at hiding things," she admitted, smiling weakly. "You know that."

She felt his slight movement, an involuntary shrinking away from her. Hayley looked at him with bewildered eyes.

But his gaze was full of passion. His mouth came down on hers, hungry and impatient. "I love you," he muttered fiercely.

His tongue was exploring her with tantalizingly eager twists that left her breathless. But her mind clammered uneasily. He sounded *determined* to love her, as if he were fighting impossible odds. But that was crazy, wasn't it? She'd been the one who'd had doubts about their relationship.

"God, Hayley . . ."

If she'd doubted his desire, those doubts washed away like water over smooth stone. His hand was pressed urgently against the small of her back, his body hard with longing against hers.

They slid as one to the floor, muscles straining, mouths still clinging. Kennedy slung a leg over her, his ravenous mouth searching out the remembered hollows of her throat, the trembling eagerness of her breasts.

"Help me," he muttered, his hands on the buttons of her dress. It was swirled out beneath her like a white, ravaged cape. She undid the buttons with quick fingers, half-afraid whatever demon Kennedy was fighting would tear him away from her before she could love him.

Then she was naked and helping him off with his clothes. The shirt came off with a swift, muscular twist. She fumbled for the zip of his pants and he guided her hands. Her breath caught at his involuntary groan.

"Hayley . . . beautiful, beautiful, Hayley . . ."

His weight covered her. It was all she needed. Wrapping herself around him, loving him, she felt him poised above her in a kind of terrifying indecision.

"What is it?" she whispered fearfully. "Kennedy . . ."

His face was pressed against her neck, then a terrible shudder wracked him. The next second she thought she'd imagined it as, with one swift movement, his body was joined to hers.

"I love you, Hayley," he said thickly, and she had the feeling there was far more to his words she might ever know.

"Then love me . . . just love me . . ."

He moved slowly, savoring the incredible tightness of her, stroking with an exquisite slowness that brought Hayley trembling on the brink of sensation within seconds. She moaned softly, the world exploding as she came apart in his arms, her desire bringing an answering shudder from Kennedy as he poured himself out to her, a slave to the frightening depths of his own love for her.

Hayley tipped her chin up to the sun, legs crossed negligently at the ankles, as she surveyed the view of ceaseless slate-blue ocean and hazy afternoon sky from Kennedy's back deck. She peeled off a section of orange, laughing as she accidentally squirted him with the juice.

"I could get used to this," she said, closing her eyes contentedly.

And she could. Very used to it. Making love to Kennedy, whiling away an entire morning in his arms, enjoying quiet moments with him under a warm, yellow sun—it was paradise for a lonely Oregonian

who'd just passed through four of the most miserable
months of her life.

Kennedy's head was bent in concentration as he
peeled another orange. His silence penetrated
Hayley's cocoon of self-indulgence.

"Hey," she said softly, that little prickle of worry
skittering down her spine. "It's time to 'fess up.
What's weighing you down?"

Kennedy drew a deep breath of sea air into his
lungs. He wondered what he could tell her that
wouldn't spoil the mood between them.

Hayley saw the deep grooves that tightened beside
his mouth. "Is it that bad? You've just spent hours
convincing me it isn't me. Can't you tell me what it
is?"

Kennedy's distress was like a rock in his stomach.
He held out another section of orange to her but she
shook her head, wisps of hair tossed across her face
from the breeze. Her concern was real, and anguished, beneath her light tone.

"Gordon Woodrow stopped by this morning," he
said at length. "He's Titan Pictures' head of production."

"I know who he is." He had her full attention now.
She knew instinctively it had something to do with
Claudia Jeffries's suit against him.

Kennedy's gaze was on the horizon, his eyes narrowed against the glare. "Gordon's a worrier. And
he's notorious for dropping his opinion on you, generally when you need it the least."

"What has he said?" Her insides were filling with
dread.

"Lots." Kennedy turned his attention on her. "He's not a fan of Sinclair, Holmsby, and Layton."

It was something she'd already known, or at least guessed. She didn't see that it was so inherently bad, however; Kennedy had to have known Gordon's feelings from the onset.

"I take it he objects to your seeing me," Hayley remarked, slipping on her sunglasses.

Kennedy didn't like the way that sounded. Thinking he was making a mistake in even trying to explain, he growled, "I've never put much stock in Gordon's opinions. I'm not going to start now."

Hayley said nothing, but she knew that if Gordon had made Kennedy reassess his feelings for her, he'd had doubts himself. She felt suddenly naked and vulnerable, her buried insecurities rising swiftly to the surface.

"But . . . ?" Tension was stretched between them like a hair-fine wire.

Kennedy's chair squeaked as he shifted his weight. Hayley couldn't look at him. *Here it comes,* she thought fatalistically. *Here it comes.*

He was silent for long seconds, eons. All sound ceased for Hayley. She scarcely breathed.

"I'd like to ask you a question. You don't have to answer if you feel it's a breach of confidence—considering Claudia Jeffries is appealing."

Confused, Hayley turned her head to search his face.

"Who," Kennedy asked grimly, "at your firm, advised Claudia Jeffries to go to trial?"

Whatever she'd expected, this wasn't it. "No

one," she answered. "It was Claudia's decision. Why?"

"Didn't you try to talk her into settling?"

"Well, yes. Of course."

"But she went ahead anyway."

Hayley proceeded with extreme caution. She had the sensation of being led into a trap. She shrugged lightly. "You know Claudia."

She saw his hand scour his chin, fingers stiff with tension. "If something had gone wrong during the trial—if a mistrial had been claimed, for instance. Or . . . if she lost . . ."

Like she did . . . Hayley couldn't stand the suspense. "Yes?"

Kennedy shook his head. "It was just a lot chancier than a settlement, that's all. I'm surprised she'd choose that route."

Hayley looked at him oddly. "Did you think someone at our office gave her that advice?"

His green eyes stared at her. "Yes."

Hayley smiled. "Not a chance. The risk of losing was too high. And, let's face it, that's just what happened. No one benefited from the trial but you."

A scowl darkened Kennedy's features, matching the direction of his thoughts. Someone else had counted on benefiting—someone in Hayley's firm. That someone had wanted to ally with the other side, and reap a hefty fee in the bargain. Forcing the case to go to trial would increase the chances for Claudia to lose—and Kennedy to win.

Was Hayley telling the truth? The agony of not knowing was tearing his guts out.

Realizing he was putting off the inevitable, hating himself for it, Kennedy abruptly changed the subject. "Gordon wants us to come to a screening of *Pleasure Hunt* tomorrow night. I promised we'd go before you catch your flight back."

Hayley felt as if he'd closed a door in her face. Whatever was bothering him was yet to be resolved. "Okay." Kennedy reached a hand across to her, and she turned her cheek toward his palm, watching him with wide, vulnerable eyes.

"Oh, love," he murmured, moving with quick grace to join her on the lounge chair. A protesting groan sounded ominously beneath them.

"Be careful." Her words were filled with silent laughter. "We'll break it."

The sound of splintering wood punctuated her remark. Neither one of them moved a muscle. They stared at one another, gray eyes bare inches from green. It was a delicious kind of forced stillness, and Hayley could feel Kennedy's potent maleness growing in spite of it.

"What," she whispered, eyes dancing, "do you think we should do?"

"Nothing." His gaze dropped longingly to her mouth. "Oh, God . . ."

Hayley fought the urge to move against his seductive weight, sensing their precarious balance keenly. Her eyes flashed with humor. "It's your move," she murmured.

A dangerous glint entered his eyes. Then, with a sudden twist he was off the chair, pulling her up with steel-muscled arms. "Let's go find something with a sturdier base."

"Such as?" Hayley laughed.

"A bed, or the floor, or anywhere else." He swooped her into his arms, and carried her back into the house. "I've only got a few hours left with you," he said on a more serious note. "I intend to make the most of them."

Hayley's laughter died beneath the burning hunger of his gaze. When he bent to kiss her neck, her head lolled back, her body turning to liquid. But something —that something she couldn't quite get a handle on—bothered her.

I've only got a few hours left with you.

It almost sounded as if he meant something other than just an end to her weekend stay.

"Kennedy . . . ?"

His mouth was foraying to the straining button that held her dress together above her breasts. He tugged on it with his teeth, coming down beside her on the bed.

"Hmmm?"

He wasn't really listening. She wasn't thinking. The whole world spiraled to a narrow vortex where all she could think about were his hands, and his mouth, and the sweet pressure of his body meshed to hers.

Titan Pictures' soundstages, executive offices, screening rooms, and back lots were a group of buildings in west Los Angeles, about an hour's drive from Kennedy's home. A concrete skyway connected the parking lot with the main building, and Hayley walked beside Kennedy as he led the way across, four lanes of heavy traffic rushing beneath them.

Twilight was turning the buildings and roadways into a million glittering lights—the daylight's ugliness cloaked in an unreal glamour, as manufactured as any Hollywood film. But Hayley enjoyed the illusion, feeling a kind of bittersweet longing, a sadness that had everything to do with the fact she had to leave in just a few more hours.

Halfway across, she tugged on Kennedy's hand. "Wait," she begged. "I don't want to go in there yet."

"Gordon's not all bad," Kennedy assured her, misinterpreting her reluctance. "Just ninety-nine percent." His grin slashed brilliantly in the gathering darkness. "But I'm sure you could win him over if you tried."

"I don't know. He sounds like he's full of prejudice against me."

They'd avoided the issue of the trial since Kennedy's terse questions the day before. He'd seemed to have come to some kind of unspoken decision, and Hayley was just glad the crisis was past. She believed he would tell her what had been bothering him when the time was right. Maybe it had all been in her mind anyway, a product of her anxiety-riddled brain. Whatever, it didn't seem to matter anymore.

"Gordon's always looking out for his own interests," Kennedy said, looking down at the traffic. "He

sees people as either for him, or against him, and
that's all. There are no gray areas in business."

Hayley regarded Kennedy curiously. "And what
are you, to him? Besides a moneymaking director."

Kennedy made a sound of self-mockery between his
teeth. "Nothing, most likely. Our friendship doesn't
really go beyond business."

"I get the feeling this is leading somewhere."

Kennedy didn't smile. The breeze whipped strands
of Hayley's hair across his cheek and he brushed them
back, meditatively watching as they slid, burnished
gold, between his fingers. "I'm not as black and white
as Gordon," he said, his jaw working. "At least not
about people, and what they can do for me. I'm more
emotional than that."

This admission surprised and baffled her. "Creative
people usually are," she murmured noncommittally.
Premonition was prickling the skin on her arms.
Something was coming, that something she'd been
worrying about all weekend, she guessed. Suddenly,
irrationally, she didn't want to know what it was.

She shivered as Kennedy went on, "And when it
comes to you—anything to do with you—I'd be the
first to admit that I can't be objective."

Hayley rubbed her elbows with her palms, cold and
anxious. "You're scaring me, Kennedy."

He shook his head, half-angry. "There's something
going on in your company," he said abruptly, furious
with his own caution. He'd been putting this off all
weekend. It was time to stop fooling himself and
Hayley.

"Someone at Sinclair, Holmsby, and Layton offered to sell information about my case to Titan Pictures," he said flatly.

Hayley blinked, her mouth curving tentatively upward at his absurdity. *"What?"* His expression didn't alter, and fear clouded her brain. "Don't be ridiculous," she said instantly, scathingly.

"I'm not." Defeat scored lines of unhappiness down his cheeks.

"It's not true. No one would—" Hayley clenched her teeth together. "You know as well as I do, Kennedy, that no one at Sinclair, Holmsby, and Layton would do such a thing! It would defeat the whole purpose of the trial." She squared her shoulders. "Who supposedly tried to make this arrangement?"

Her outrage didn't make Kennedy feel any better. "Titan doesn't know who made the offer. It was done anonymously."

Hayley felt like she'd been kicked in the stomach. She suddenly saw everything with brutal clarity. Color drained from her face at the implications. "It's a mistake," she whispered harshly.

Kennedy's shoulders ached with strain. "That was my initial reaction." Then, tiredly, he continued, "It's no mistake."

Hayley took a step backward, pushing up a restraining hand as Kennedy moved with her. He froze immediately, his face ravaged with emotion.

"You think I did it," she said, surprised at how conversational she sounded when she was dying inside.

"I don't—"

"Yes . . . yes, you do." Her whisper was rough with betrayal, "My God," she moaned. "Oh, oh, God . . ." Her stomach revolted and she clutched it protectively with one arm, backing away.

Kennedy's face was pale. "Hayley, listen to me—"

"No." Her hair tumbled in violent disarray as she shook her head. "You're so *wrong.*"

"I don't know who did it," Kennedy bit out tersely, quickly, alarmed by her reaction. "I need your help to find out. You need to know, love. Your father needs—"

"That's why you asked me all those questions about the trial." Her mind suddenly cleared. "You aren't even concerned about the appeal."

"I'm concerned about you," Kennedy said tautly.

Hayley could hardly breathe. Her lungs were aching, starving for air. "Is that why you invited me down here? To discover the truth? To drag a confession from me?"

"No!"

Hayley was shaking. "Is that why you made love to me?" she demanded in a high, thin voice. She recognized her own rising hysteria but didn't care.

"I love you," he said fiercely.

"Go to hell, Kennedy." She turned blindly away, struggling when his hands clamped on her shoulders.

"You think I wanted to tell you this! My God, Hayley! I've been sick inside since Gordon told me the truth."

"The *truth?*" Hayley's body was a rigid plank. She hunched her shoulders against his touch. "You certainly have audacity," she said bitterly. "Accusing me of selling out my own father and naming it the truth. Let go of me!"

She twisted from him, but this time Kennedy wasn't going to let her run out on him. He grabbed her roughly and spun her to face him, glaring into her frigid gray eyes.

"What I'm saying is the truth." He fought the urge to shake her once, hard. "Someone at your company is trying to make money on the side. Damn it, Hayley! I don't know who it is. But it's not my problem, is it? It's yours! Yours and your company's. Don't you even want to know?"

"All I want is to get out," she said through white lips.

Kennedy groaned, pulling her stiff body against his, fighting her coldness with his heat. "I love you," he muttered harshly.

Hayley felt herself screaming inside. *Meaningless words. Meaningless, meaningless words* . . .

"Hayley . . ."

"People who really love one another, trust one another." Hayley's throat was hot and hurting. She could barely whisper. "You don't know how to love, Kennedy. It's all a script to you, a fantasy. A few well-chosen words and the hero wins the girl. Well that's not the way it works!"

She had ceased fighting. She heard his tattered breathing, sensed his despair, knew the warmth and need of his embrace, but felt nothing. Nothing but an empty void.

And Kennedy could feel her pulling away to a place he couldn't follow.

"I'm losing you," he said, his voice barely audible, thick with misery.

Tears fought their way up her throat but she held them down. She eased herself from his strong arms, her emotional distance shattering his hope. She'd never seen him look so vulnerable.

"Hayley . . ."

The pain he'd inflicted fortified her against his gaunt, ravaged face. Pivoting away, she hit back with the only artillery she had left.

"You can't lose what you never had, Mr. Taft." The words choked her but she said them again, enunciating carefully, "You can't lose what you never had. . . ."

Chapter Twelve

Hayley's apartment looked bleak and dreary after the sunlit extravaganza of Kennedy's beach-front home. But it represented a curious kind of warmth from the cold desolation that had invaded her soul. She still couldn't believe he could be that horribly wrong about her.

Hayley walked directly to the fireplace, stacking it with wood and setting a match to the dry tinder. She shivered uncontrollably even after the blaze was bright and hot, aftershocks of Kennedy's betrayal.

She hadn't been able to think of anything but her misery on the plane. She was still too hurt to be angry. How could he think that of her? How *could* he? Four months of being separated couldn't alter one's opinion that much.

Hayley closed her eyes and rubbed her temples. She

was feeling low enough to believe he'd never really cared for her the way he'd professed. He'd never really loved her.

And maybe she hadn't loved him. Maybe it had all been a grand illusion, a way to justify her attraction to a man totally unlike herself, a man incapable of loving her.

Hayley sighed deeply, slowly reopening her eyes and gazing morosely into the flames. A grim smile tightened her lips. *And that,* she told herself, *is a lovely rationale. Unfortunately, it just isn't true.*

Even after everything she loved him. Still.

Being with Kennedy in California had been wonderful. If he'd asked, she would have given up her life in Portland and moved to Los Angeles—that's how much she loved him. She would have packed in reality and followed a dream—that's how much she loved him. She would have given him all of herself, asking nothing in return—that's how much she loved him.

A secret, hopeful part of her had wanted him to ask her to make the move; she'd been prepared to say yes without hesitation.

But he hadn't asked . . . and now she knew why.

How could he think that of her? She balled her hands into fists and raged impotently, anger quickly disintegrating to despair. How could he listen to Gordon Woodrow about something he knew to be untrue? *How could he?*

Hayley walked into the kitchen, gloomily noticing how lousy the weather was. The wind was howling, branches rattling against the window. As much as she told herself she was glad to be back in Oregon, the gray, oppressive weather mocked her.

She switched on her answering machine to distract her from her own wretched thoughts. Her mind was already playing tricks on her, looking for possibilities to misinterpret what Kennedy had meant. But inside she knew. *She knew.*

The first message was from her father, asking her to call him when she got back. Hayley pressed the advance button, resolutely pushing thoughts of Kennedy Taft and a warm, seductive California night from her mind. The second call was from Matthew.

"Hello, Hayley. Where are you? The Wilson trial's Monday, y'know. Call me as soon as you get in."

There was something disturbing in that message, an undertone of anxiety that threaded through Matthew's voice. Hayley's brow knit, then she shook her head. She was jumping at shadows.

She forged ahead. A frantic voice said, "Hello, Miss Sinclair? It's Tom Wilson. I need to talk to you. *Immediately.* We've got problems and the trial's tomorrow." A pause, then tensely, "I'll be waiting for your call."

Hayley groaned, her shoulders slumping. What kind of problems now? She stabbed the button and heard the last message.

"I hope you're listening to me," Kennedy's disembodied voice warned, "because I'm tired of being cut off. I love you. I *still* love you. But I'm doing my damnedest to get over you. It should be easy, after the way you've run out on me—twice. But things are never that simple, are they?" She heard him mutter something under his breath before he continued. "When you come to your senses call me," he added, his hurt buried beneath a powerful anger.

"Arrogant bastard," Hayley whispered in disbelief. But she played the tape again.

When you come to your senses call me.

She felt like killing him! When *she* came to *her* senses! My God! He was beyond belief.

Hayley stared at the machine. An uncomfortable twinge of guilt reminded her she *had* run out on him. Oh, he'd taken her to the airport all right, but she'd been fleeing. She couldn't remember what he'd said to her during the ride; she'd been too self-absorbed. Maybe he hadn't said anything. It certainly didn't matter now.

When you come to your senses . . .

Hayley sat in one of the ladder-back kitchen chairs, feeling oddly off-balance. She hadn't really given much thought to Kennedy's accusations—other than that they were meant for her. She'd simply rejected the idea that anyone at Sinclair, Holmsby, and Layton would do something so unethical. It just couldn't be.

Now, she reconsidered. *Was* it possible? Could someone at the firm really have sent that message to Titan? Did the message even exist? Or was it all an elaborate hoax, maybe even an out-and-out lie manufactured by Titan executives?

She was trying objectively to put herself in Kennedy's shoes and look at the situation from his angle, when her doorbell chimed.

Kennedy! Hayley was out of the chair before her irrationality hit her. She was horrified at herself.

"It's not Kennedy," she muttered furiously. "He's still in California, and you don't want to see him anyway, remember?"

Depressed, Hayley realized how tragically often she would have to remind herself.

"Matthew," Hayley said, startled, as the door swung inward at the twist of her hand.

"Didn't you get my message?" he asked, stepping inside as Hayley motioned for him to come in.

"Well, yes, but I just got back." Hayley surreptitiously glanced at the clock, wondering what urgency had forced Matthew out tonight.

Matthew's eyes darted around her apartment, as if he expected something, or someone, to be lurking in the corners. He swiped at his hair with restless fingers.

The uneasy feeling she'd gotten after hearing his message returned. Hayley shot him a worried look. "Is something wrong, Matthew?" she asked. His face was scored by haggard lines. New ones, she was sure.

"Wrong?" He made a deprecating noise. "You mean worse than usual?"

"Is it Sheryl?" she asked carefully. Kennedy's allegations were fresh in her mind, and, rather unfairly, she couldn't help wondering about Matthew. Could he be the one? Would he really sell out the firm? If, indeed, someone from Sinclair, Holmsby, and Layton had asked for a bribe?

Her own thoughts horrified her. Matthew? What was she thinking of! He was her closest friend at the firm, her most unfailing ally. It frightened her, how far she would go to believe Kennedy.

"Hardly." Matthew's mouth slanted bitterly. "I think," he said heavily, "I'm about to be fired."

Hayley was shocked. "Why? What for?"

He just shook his head, looking crumpled and defeated. She noticed the trembling of his hands and wondered anxiously if he'd been drinking.

He sighed. "I got a really nasty client mad at me. Your father—"

The shrill ring of the phone shushed Matthew instantly. His eyes flared in alarm, and Hayley's concern heightened.

"My father, what?" she asked quickly, ignoring the phone. A thrill of apprehension shot up her spine. She wondered if the call was from Kennedy.

Two rings. Three.

Matthew seemed to gather himself for a moment, then he frowned, his mouth tightening. The seconds stretched. With a sound of exasperation, Hayley grabbed for the phone.

"Hello?" she asked, heart pounding.

"Miss Sinclair." Tom Wilson's voice was flat and angry. "Didn't you get my message? I'm desperate to talk to you."

"I—yes—Mr. Wilson. I know." Hayley drew in a deep breath, hiding her disappointment. Of course Kennedy wouldn't call. She knew that. He wouldn't call her—she was supposed to call him.

Her fingers tightened around the receiver. She seemed fated to have everything always happen at once. "I was just going to call you," she went on. "What's the problem?"

"Hayley."

Matthew's urgent tone caused her to turn and look at him. She signaled impatiently that she would be off in a minute.

Matthew ignored her. His face was ghostly white. "I'll catch you later," he muttered, on his way to the door. "When you're not so busy."

"Just a minute." Hayley cut Tom Wilson off before he could make a point. "Excuse me," she hastily apologized, aware that she was probably agitating the man to the point of demanding a new lawyer. But one thing at a time . . .

"Matthew, wait. I'll be right—" Hayley twisted away from the phone, craning to see him. The door to her apartment shut with a slam.

"Miss Sinclair?" Tom Wilson's tone was ice.

"I'm sorry, Mr. Wilson, I had a friend here who just left. Please go on with what you were saying."

Hayley sank into the chair next to the phone, staring blankly at the front door. She was nonplussed, and a bit worried, by Matthew's behavior. What had he been going to say about her father?

". . . leaking information about my case. I know it sounds preposterous, but it's a fact. Computektron knows my every move. I have friends that are still there, Miss Sinclair. One of them overheard some very damaging information, and he's passed it on to me."

Hayley's attention was yanked back to her client.

"What are you saying?" she asked, her breath stopping.

"I'm saying, someone at your office hasn't kept their mouth shut." His outrage emanated over the wire. "What the hell kind of firm are you? I was willing to believe the hullabaloo over the Taft case was just smoke. Now I'm not so sure!"

"Mr. Wilson—" Hayley's hand was at her throat.

"I don't give a damn for your apologies. Save them for your next client. You'd just better not lose this case for me."

"I assure you, I don't know what you're talking about."

Hayley's tone was determined but her conscience pricked her. *Did* she know? Had Kennedy's accusations been correct?

"Don't you?" Tom Wilson was grim and controlled. "Your voice reeks of insincerity, Miss Sinclair. I hope you're a better actress in tomorrow's courtroom."

Hayley felt weak. The blood was draining from her head. "No one at our firm would stoop to such unethical practices. We prefer to win cases, Mr. Wilson."

"So your track record led me to believe. But just recently, things have changed, haven't they?" He made a pungent sound. "See you tomorrow," he threw out in disgust. The receiver slammed in her ear.

Hayley was trembling all over. Her conviction had dissolved to doubt, doubt to a terrible reality. Someone was leaking, no, *selling*, information. Someone with access. Someone without principle.

Her fingers pressed against her lips in anguish.

Who? It was someone who knew Hayley's cases intimately, so that ruled out quite a few members of the firm. It also narrowed the field to a mere handful of possibilities, chief among those Matthew Andrews and her father.

It was not Jason Sinclair. Hayley would have staked her life on that.

But Matthew?

Hayley was cold, cold down to her very soul. She moved with measured slowness into the kitchen, turning on a pot of tea, trying to warm herself from the burner. Matthew had flaws; she'd be the first to admit it. But he'd never struck her as the type of man who would do anything for money. With Matt, money wasn't an issue, or at least she didn't think it was. His only passion was his wife.

It didn't make sense.

She recalled his words. "I got a really nasty client mad at me. Your father—"

Her breath caught. Her father, *what?*

Hayley poured herself a cup of tea, her breath coming in anxious gasps. No. She would not have her mind poisoned against her own father! She knew, to the very core of her being, her self, that he was not responsible.

"No . . ." Her head wagged painfully back and forth. "No . . . oh no . . ."

The tea scalded her tongue but Hayley barely noticed. Sifting through the fragments of her memory, she recalled something else, a conversation she'd unwittingly overheard.

Matthew, talking to someone over the telephone:

"I'm trying but you've got to give me a little more time." Then, later, "They're trying to take the case away from me. . . ."

Matthew had been talking about the reverse-discrimination suit. The Tom Wilson case.

"Oh, my God," she whispered.

She sank heavily into a chair, covering her face with her hands. She had to decide what to do, and she had to decide tonight. The Wilson trial started the next day at eleven o'clock.

Kennedy jockeyed the rental car into the only available parking space within three blocks. Rain poured in uneven sheets down the windshield, obscuring everything but the blurry lights that bravely outlined the carved stone steps leading to Hayley's apartment.

You're out of your mind, he reminded himself for the thousandth time. *Completely out of your mind.*

But if permanent insanity was the only way to have Hayley, so be it. He loved her. He wanted her. And, damn it all, he intended to have her!

She hadn't written that letter to Titan.

He'd known it while Gordon had been carefully laying out the facts, but he'd listened anyway. Foolishly. But a few hours away from her, with only the company of his own morbid thoughts, had made him see the truth. He was ashamed he'd ever doubted Hayley. How could he have imagined she was capable of something like that? He *knew* Hayley, knew her feelings, her desires, her motivations. . . . For a wild few hours he'd listened to Gordon Woodrow's warped philosophy and now he was paying a terrible price. He wouldn't blame her if she slammed the door in his face.

He'd never made it to the screening of *Pleasure Hunt*. After dropping Hayley at the airport, he'd driven like a maniac back to his house, furious, desperate, out of control like he'd never been before.

The house was empty, full of echoing aloneness. Kennedy had never noticed it before, but the silence battered at him with a drowning, mocking force that had left him stunned.

He'd been angry at first, giving in to an emotional binge he hadn't thought himself capable of. He was furious at Hayley, at himself, but mostly at the incredible reality that he didn't want to live without her. He'd phoned her when his fury had been the strongest—her cool, taped voice making something shift inside him that felt very much like desolation.

The decision to go after her had taken a little longer, after he'd begun to see things the right way around. And then he'd strongly debated the wisdom of chasing after her; he'd had enough rejection to last him a lifetime.

He'd been boarding the airplane before he'd really considered what he would do if she turned him away. By the time he'd landed in Portland he'd reminded himself of all the reasons he shouldn't follow after her—then forgotten them. He loved her. Period. And he'd never get her back without trying.

Now, as he mounted the stairs, head bent against the slashing wind and rain, Kennedy steeled himself for another painful encounter. His ego had already suffered irreparable damage, yet he knew with burning certainty that Hayley cared for him, loved him; and though his suspicions had wounded her, he suspected that her love hadn't died. His teeth clenched. At least that's what he kept telling himself.

He rapped on her door, watching the rain running in rivers from the choked gutters. He couldn't hear her footsteps for the noise, and when the door swung inward, he was momentarily at a loss. Hayley's face was flooded with a rapid succession of emotions.

Heavily, wondering what he would do if she said no, Kennedy asked quietly, "May I come in?"

To his surprise tears pooled in her eyes. "You didn't wait for me to come to my senses," she said, after a long moment.

His relief was enormous. No door slamming, no hurtful accusations. "It doesn't matter," he said, wishing he could take her in his arms. "I came to mine."

He crossed the threshold and Hayley closed the door, the quick look of appreciation she sent him rapidly fading into something else. She was afraid to trust him again.

Her sigh was full of resignation but the uncertain lift to the corners of her mouth gave him hope. "Well, I'm not sure I've yet come to mine," she admitted. Then, with devastating honesty, she said, "I need you to help me."

"Any way I can, love."

Her lashes fluttered, unconsciously vulnerable, achingly beautiful. Kennedy waited, his breath held.

"I think," she said, licking dry lips, "that maybe you were right."

Kennedy remained motionless.

"Someone at the firm's been leaking information about my latest case." Hayley swallowed hard. "And I think I know who it is."

"Oh, love . . ."

"It's Matthew," she whispered. "It's got to be."

Kennedy could stand it no longer. He wrapped his arms around her, offering comfort, feeling the turbulence of her emotions, the betrayal that seethed beneath the pain. For a devastating moment he felt her stiffen, as if she couldn't forgive him for thinking it might have been her. Then she sagged against him, burying her face in the wet folds of his overcoat.

He kissed the sun-streaked gold in her hair. "I love you, Hayley. I haven't stopped."

She only huddled closer, seeking his warmth. At that moment, Kennedy was a haven of security to Hayley—not the enemy, but the only friendly port in a terrible storm. She couldn't think anymore tonight.

She turned her face up to meet his kisses, feeling his lips capture hers. "Stay with me tonight," she begged softly. "I need you."

"Always, love." Kennedy held her tightly, swaying slightly, seductively. "I'm not leaving you again. You're not leaving me."

His words were welcome, everything she needed. They continued for a long, long time, a soft croon that lulled her gently, helping her put off the horrors of reality.

"I love you," she whispered.

She hoped that, in the end, that would be enough.

The law offices of Sinclair, Holmsby, and Layton formally opened at nine each morning, but calls were accepted as early as seven-thirty. However, the phone was ringing at the ungodly hour of six A.M. as Hayley unlocked the outside door, and she debated whether to answer it or not. Who in their right mind would expect someone to be in so early?

A weight settled in Hayley's stomach. Tom Wilson might. Especially if he'd tried to reach her at home.

She resolutely picked up the receiver. "Hello?"

"Just wanted you to know that everything's going to be fine today," Kennedy's voice assured her with a sexy drawl. "I know it. So stop worrying."

For some insane reason Hayley felt herself blushing. He could make her feel so good. "I wish Tom Wilson had the confidence in me that you do."

"You've got a strong case, love. Give it your best shot." A telling pause. "Just don't think about anything else."

She knew what he meant, all the possible ramifications that were hanging in the wings. If information had indeed been leaked, either side could call a mistrial. Everything she and Tom were working for could be in vain, and her father's firm could take a real beating in credibility. The whole trial could be a travesty.

"I'll remember," Hayley promised lightly.

"Meet me at the Den tonight?"

Hayley hesitated. Generally, after the first day of a trial, she liked to unwind at home. There would be a lot of people she knew at the Den, people she might rather avoid. Yet, she couldn't hide her love for Kennedy forever.

"I'll see you there," she said, trying to allay her anxieties.

Ten minutes later she heard someone come into the office. Hayley's grip on her pen tightened as she wondered who it might be. She saw the shadow through the crack beneath her door and waited in a kind of frozen expectance.

"Hayley?" Matthew tapped lightly on her door.

Hayley set her pen down and stared blankly at the notes she'd written to herself. The Wilson case had taken on unreal proportions, yet she had no real evidence that any wrongdoing had occurred—not like the letter Gordon Woodrow had. Still, she carefully gathered the papers together and stuffed them in her briefcase. She refused to take chances. "Come on in, Matthew," she said levelly. The time for the confrontation had come.

She barely gave him time to step inside her office when she attacked. Courtroom tactics had never served their purpose better.

"Before you speak, let me say I know about what you tried to do with Titan Pictures," she said flatly. "I know about the letter. I know that, had Claudia Jeffries won, Kennedy Taft could have called a mistrial.

"Furthermore," she went on ruthlessly, "I'm aware that you may be leaking information to Computektron, therefore jeopardizing my current case. I have no proof of that yet, but I'm working on it. I'm going to find out everything, Matthew. Be assured of that."

His jaw dropped in silent protest. He started to answer, then stopped, swallowing. It was all Hayley had to see.

He sighed, his mouth tightening. "You've got it all wrong."

"Don't, Matthew. We both know better."

He shook his head vehemently. "I didn't think that Taft would tell you, that's all. I have to give the man credit. He took a chance."

Hayley held Matthew's gaze. "What are you talking about?" she asked flatly.

Matthew threw up his hands. "Maybe I should ask you that! What's all this about Computektron? I'm in the dark."

Hayley was experienced enough to know when someone was throwing the issue back at her, parrying the thrust of her argument by diffusing it. "Get back to Kennedy Taft."

Matthew's brows pulled together. "What about him?"

"What did you think he told me?"

Matthew's face changed. "Look, Hayley, maybe I was out of line. . . ."

"Stop it, Matthew." Hayley was determined. "I don't have time for this."

"Well, knowing how you feel about him . . ." Matthew pinched his lower lip between his fingers.

"I'm more concerned about you right now." Her

voice was unrelenting, punishing. She intended to push the truth out of him before he had time to think.

But inside Hayley felt a nebulous panic, a dim reaction to Matthew's allusions that made her feel the ground she'd thought secure was suddenly riddled with traps.

"It was Taft's idea," Matthew said sullenly. "He offered me money to keep him informed."

Hayley was ripped by a bolt of pure terror before she came to her senses. "You tried to strike a deal with Titan," she reminded him tersely, "not Kennedy Taft."

Matthew nodded. "The Titan deal was second, after the one with Taft," he added pointedly. Lifting defeated shoulders, Matthew went on, "I figured, what the hell? I was already in over my head anyway."

"I don't believe you."

Matthew fixed her with a knowing eye. "How come I knew you'd feel that way?"

"Why, Matthew? *Why?*" All the implications crashed down on Hayley like an enormous, powerful wave.

For the first time Matthew actually looked contrite. "I don't know. Really. Money, maybe." He inhaled a deep breath. "I don't suppose I was actually thinking straight."

Because she had to, because it was the only thing that made sense, Hayley began to see. "This all happened when you were first separated from Sheryl."

Matthew shoved his hands into his pockets and looked away. "Uh . . . yeah . . ."

Hayley felt sick, sick with the truth, sick with herself.

"The things we do for love." Matthew was mocking. "We're two of a kind, y'know. Both easy targets. Look how Taft got to you."

She still didn't believe Kennedy was part of it. It was too easy for Matthew to shift blame.

As if reading her thoughts, he said, "He deliberately planned to seduce you, Hayley. He told me. I hate to admit it, because I never intended to hurt you, but I was instrumental in setting up that first meeting at the Den between the two of you."

Hayley's convictions were wavering; they couldn't stand such a brutal attack. But she refused to argue. She knew the chances of losing.

"Just like you said," Matthew went on. "He figured he'd claim a mistrial if he lost."

"My relationship with Kennedy began after the trial," Hayley said through white lips.

"Hayley, sweetheart. Don't kid yourself." His face, though white and scared, was full of unwanted empathy. "Look where it's gotten me!"

Fear was flooding through her. Doubt was taking root. Her insides seemed to be flowing away. "I think we've said enough, Matthew."

Matthew suddenly bounded to his feet. He stabbed a finger in front of her face. "I'm not going down alone!" he yelled. "Taft's responsible and if you can't follow through, I can!"

Shaken, Hayley asked, "What does that mean?"

"You still don't believe me, do you?" Matthew's mouth worked in anger. "What will it take to convince you?" he demanded, then, rapid-fire, "What about when Claudia Jeffries found you two at the Cheswick? Do you really think that was an *accident?*"

Hayley's nails dug into her palm. With practiced calm, she asked, "How else could she have known?"

"Taft told her."

"No. It was pure, dumb, miserable luck." Hayley held a startled breath. "Unless you told her, Matthew. You had a pretty good idea where I was going that night."

"You've really got me painted black, don't you?" Matthew bit out angrily. "Listen to me. Claudia Jeffries is no friend of mine."

"I can't believe anything you say!"

Hayley heard the shrill sound of her own voice and recognized it for what it was: denial. Bitter, bitter denial.

"All right!" Agitated fingers ran through his hair. "I made a deal with Claudia too."

"Oh, Lord." Hayley let herself sink even further into her chair. She wasn't prepared to cope with this—not all of this! Belatedly, she realized she should have gone to her father before confronting Matthew.

"Claudia wanted more ammunition in her court fight. She paid me to help her. I thought she could win." His arm reached to Hayley in entreaty. "No matter what happened, I thought you could pull this one off. You're brilliant in the courtroom, Hayley. I figured she'd be better off going to trial."

Hayley's face was carved in stone. But, beneath,

the granite emotions were shifting and splintering, moving and hurting.

"You talked her out of settling?" she asked in a dead voice.

Matthew's mouth thinned. "She was all for going for the big bucks. You know Claudia."

"Better than I know you, obviously." Hayley's voice was a thread of pain.

"Hayley . . ." Matthew was truly wounded.

She linked her fingers together on the top of her desk, knuckles white with distress. "I have to ask myself why you're telling me all of this now," she said in a reasonable voice. It was almost a charade, playacting. It couldn't be real. "You didn't have to. So, I can only assume you thought telling me would be the safest way out."

Matthew said nothing. He just waited, his eyes pinned to hers.

"If you thought I'd keep it under wraps, you're wrong."

Panic slid across Matthew's face for the briefest of seconds.

"I can't, Matthew," Hayley went on. "I'm going straight to my father. And if you purposely implicated Kennedy with the thought that that would sway me, you were wrong about that too."

"You'd like it to be that simple, wouldn't you!" Matthew's immobility suddenly turned to trembling rage. "You'd love me to shoulder all the blame and let your precious lover off the hook. Well, too bad, Hayley. Kennedy Taft's in this up to his eyeballs! What have you told *him* about the Wilson case?

Maybe he's decided to make a little extra that way too!"

"That's absurd!"

"Yeah? Well, come up with a better idea, because I'm not taking the blame for that rap too!"

Matthew took a couple threatening steps toward her, then stopped, breathing hard. Hayley's eyes were wide with alarm but she didn't move. A moment passed, and then another. Hayley was about to collapse beneath the dreadful, silent battle of nerves when Matthew suddenly wheeled about and slammed out of her office.

Hayley felt that uncontrollable shaking get its grip on her again. It started in her legs, moved upward to her chest, then to her hands, and finally her lips. Tremors wracked her, and she felt a clawing sickness rise in her throat.

It was long minutes before she got herself under control again, but a look in the mirror confirmed her worst fears. She was white as a sheet, her pupils widened, purple circles painted around her eyes. She looked as sick as she felt.

And she had a trial that afternoon.

The jurors had all been selected; today she would give her opening statements. For the first time in her career, Hayley knew she wasn't up to it.

At eight-thirty she walked the few feet it took to get to her father's office. She had to tell him. He had to know about everything.

He wasn't in yet so she sank into one of the empty chairs, her head swimming with fears and uncertainties, her heart heavy, aching.

What if Matthew had been telling the truth?

She'd trusted Matthew, depended on him, yet he'd shown a lethal weakness. Though his actions had been prompted in part by misguided love, it made him none the less guilty. And if he could fool her, didn't it follow that Kennedy could too? Just how susceptible was she to men she cared about?

Hayley shuddered. Kennedy was not at fault. The idea that he would have anything to do with the Wilson case was preposterous. Yet . . .

Certain memories came back, unbidden, unwanted. Hayley wanted to close her mind to them, but couldn't.

There were things Kennedy had said. Innocent things, that now took on horrible double meanings.

I'm not as black and white as Gordon. She'd believed that to be a positive remark at the time, but now saw the possibility that he might not always walk the straight and narrow.

Just wanted you to know that everything's going to be fine today. The Wilson case? Hayley shook her head violently. Impossible!

Somehow I thought lawyers were always in it for the money. He'd been gently mocking her on that one, and she'd replied that she wasn't that selfless. But could it really have been a way of testing the waters? Seeing if she might actually take a bribe?

Hayley snapped her neck back, massaging tense muscles. Now she was getting crazy. That had been *after* the trial.

So what was real? What was the truth?

Hayley realized dimly that several voices, raised in

excitement, were conversing in the hallway. A moment later the door to her father's office swung inward and Jason Sinclair stood in the doorway.

"Hayley! There you are. Bernadette's been ringing your office for twenty minutes."

Hayley rose from her chair. "Oh? Why?"

"Something's breaking on the Wilson case. The press have got hold of it and accusations are flying." Her father looked harried. "Judge O'Neill is planning to postpone. Otherwise there might be grounds for a mistrial."

Hayley felt a small relief. "Does Tom Wilson know?"

"Mmm-hmm. He's in the other office, looking for you. Uh, Hayley—"

Relief gave way to dread. "Yes?"

"He's got some things he wants to talk to you about. He seems to feel Sinclair, Holmsby, and Layton is partially to blame." Her father's silver brows lifted. "Got any idea what he's talking about?"

Hayley smiled wanly. "One or two."

"Care to share them?"

Hayley sighed heavily. It was time to shift the burden, relate the events that had led to the current crisis, explain her own involvement—and Kennedy's.

"Sit down, Dad," she said wearily. "This is going to take a while, I'm afraid."

Her father nodded, his expression grave. "I've got all the time in the world. . . ."

The Den of Antiquity was nearly empty at two o'clock in the afternoon, and Hayley found a secluded booth without any trouble. She settled down for a long wait, realizing the lonely hours ahead could be the most crucial of her life.

Her father had had very little to say after she'd laid out the facts. He'd called Matthew into his office and demanded the truth from him. Matthew, looking scared but calm, had admitted his guilt, but he'd also adamantly insisted on Kennedy's involvement. After that, Jason Sinclair had quietly asked Hayley to leave.

And leave she had—out of the office, out of the building and nearly out of her mind. She knew that Matt could be deliberately lying about Kennedy's involvement. He'd shown himself capable of worse.

But what was real?

Hayley ordered a cup of coffee, staring moodily into its shimmering depths as she turned the cup in an endless circle.

Her head was muddled, her brain sluggish. She felt like she'd been worrying over Kennedy for a lifetime.

The only thing she could say for certain was that she loved him. Totally, fully, and unequivocally. And, yes, she believed that he loved her.

Yet he'd thought her involved in the information leak. That showed a lack of trust. And now she was having trouble trusting him.

Because of Matthew Andrews.

Hayley's brows knit in amazement as she considered that. How in the world could she give any credence to what Matthew said, when it was put up against Kennedy's word? There was no comparison! Even in the courtroom, when she'd first battled

Kennedy, she'd been impressed by his honesty, his assurance, his strength of character.

How could she possibly listen to Matthew?

For the next few hours, Hayley weighed her conclusions carefully. But as time went on, her conviction grew. It wasn't just what she wanted to believe. It was *what* she believed. She realized, with an ironic lift to her mouth, that she'd been guilty of losing her perspective once more.

The Den was slowly filling up with people. Hayley watched the crowds filter through, her thoughts racing madly. Now that she knew what was true, she had to do something. But what? Call her father? He would hardly listen to her about Kennedy at this juncture. He would accuse her of listening to her heart and not her head, which was exactly what she was doing.

But sometimes you have to take a chance.

There's an element of risk in everything.

When Kennedy walked in she was still sitting in the booth, the same woman who'd passed through the Den's doors earlier except for one vital difference: she believed in the man she loved.

He saw her instantly. Hayley half rose from her chair, then her knees went weak. She sank gratefully into the cushion as Kennedy slid in across from her.

"I heard," he said solemnly, before she could manage a word. "It's on the news."

"About Matt?"

He nodded, his silver-green eyes searching the depths of hers. There was an unspoken question between them. Hayley knew what it was.

"I know you weren't involved," she said simply, her faith shining from her face.

"Oh, love," Kennedy groaned, scarcely believing his good fortune.

He clasped Hayley's hands between his own. He felt humble in her trust in him, her belief and love.

He smoothed one hand over hers, memorizing the delicate bones and skin, loving her as he never had before. "Gordon Woodrow once accused me of carrying a talisman," he murmured. His eyes swept to hers, hungry and loving. "I'm beginning to believe him."

Hayley smiled, delicately soothing the lines of worry beside his mouth with her finger. "Now we just have to figure out a way to let the rest of the world know about your innocence."

Kennedy caught her finger with his lips. He nibbled gently, then said, "Gordon's taking care of that too. He's coming to Portland tomorrow with the letter on Sinclair, Holmsby, and Layton stationery."

"You think that'll be enough?"

"More than enough. Especially after Andrews's involvement in the Wilson case."

Hayley's look of astonishment surprised Kennedy. He purposely placed her hand on the table, knowing now was not the time for distractions. "Didn't you know?" he asked.

She shook her head. "Matt was still denying his involvement when I left."

"Well, he's confessed now. The whole dirty business is topping tonight's news. Computektron actually paid him, and they're in trouble deep. Wilson will probably make out like a bandit. A settlement's bound to be the next thing now."

A last regret slid over Hayley—a regret for the Matthew she'd once known. "I'm sorry," she whispered.

"So am I."

Crowds of people were filling up the intimate bar. The conversation was humming. Hayley's ears picked up the name of her firm several times.

"Everyone's talking about it," she said softly.

"Wait until they find out we're over here," Kennedy said grimly.

"What do you want to do?"

His eyes slid lazily over her face, enjoying every texture. "I don't know. Something sane and predictable and rational. Let's run off and get married."

Hayley made a choked sound, peering at him closely to read his mood. "Tonight?"

"Mmm-hmm. What d'ya say?" He leaned forward, until his nose nearly touched hers.

A smile teased her mouth. "Maybe."

His expression grew more serious. "I've always felt Southern California needs another lawyer."

"Like it needs another real estate agent?"

Kennedy brushed his lips across hers. "There's always room for excellence," he argued. "Is it a deal?"

"On one condition. We put off the wedding for a few days." At Kennedy's look of consternation, she laughed, "We couldn't get married tonight unless we flew to Nevada. Besides, I've got a better idea."

"This I gotta hear."

Out of her peripheral vision Hayley saw a lawyer from another firm nudge his friend and point in her direction. Word was spreading like wildfire.

"I never got to visit your suite at the Cheswick," she said quickly. "I thought we might go see if it's occupied, and if not . . . well, we could occupy it."

Kennedy's palms captured her face. He kissed her with an abandon generally reserved for complete privacy, causing a ripple of appreciation from the crowd. Hayley blushed crimson.

"Did anyone ever tell you you have great ideas?" he murmured.

Hayley fumbled for her purse, grinning. "Did anyone ever tell you there's a time and place for everything?"

"I flunked etiquette."

They rose from the booth simultaneously. Kennedy's hand curved possessively around Hayley's elbow.

"I love you," she whispered.

"And I love you." Kennedy held the door and growled in her ear, "Now let's get the hell out of here so I can start adding action to words."

"Beautifully put." Hayley laughed and they slipped through the door, unaware of the friendly clapping and laughing that followed from the envious patrons inside.

WIN

a fabulous $50,000 diamond jewelry collection

ENTER

by filling out the coupon below and mailing it by September 30, 1985

Send entries to:

U.S.
Silhouette Diamond Sweepstakes
P.O. Box 779
Madison Square Station
New York, NY 10159

Canada
Silhouette Diamond Sweepstakes
Suite 191
238 Davenport Road
Toronto, Ontario M5R 1J6

SILHOUETTE DIAMOND SWEEPSTAKES ENTRY FORM

☐ Mrs.   ☐ Miss   ☐ Ms   ☐ Mr.

NAME _____ (please print) _____

ADDRESS _____ APT. #

CITY _____

STATE/(PROV.) _____

ZIP/(POSTAL CODE) _____

RTD-A-1

RULES FOR SILHOUETTE DIAMOND SWEEPSTAKES

OFFICIAL RULES—NO PURCHASE NECESSARY

1. Silhouette Diamond Sweepstakes is open to Canadian (except Quebec) and United States residents 18 years or older at the time of entry. Employees and immediate families of the publishers of Silhouette, their affiliates, retailers, distributors, printers, agencies and RONALD SMILEY INC. are excluded.

2. To enter, print your name and address on the official entry form or on a 3" x 5" slip of paper. You may enter as often as you choose, but each envelope must contain only one entry. Mail entries first class in Canada to Silhouette Diamond Sweepstakes, Suite 191, 238 Davenport Road, Toronto, Ontario M5R 1J6. In the United States, mail to Silhouette Diamond Sweepstakes, P.O. Box 779, Madison Square Station, New York, NY 10159. Entries must be postmarked between February 1 and September 30, 1985. Silhouette is not responsible for lost, late or misdirected mail.

3. First Prize of diamond jewelry, consisting of a necklace, ring, bracelet and earrings will be awarded. Approximate retail value is $50,000 U.S./$62,500 Canadian. Second Prize of 100 Silhouette Home Reader Service Subscriptions will be awarded. Approximate retail value of each is $162.00 U.S./$180.00 Canadian. No substitution, duplication, cash redemption or transfer of prizes will be permitted. Odds of winning depend upon the number of valid entries received. One prize to a family or household. Income taxes, other taxes and insurance on First Prize are the sole responsibility of the winners.

4. Winners will be selected under the supervision of RONALD SMILEY INC., an independent judging organization whose decisions are final, by random drawings from valid entries postmarked by September 30, 1985, and received no later than October 7, 1985. Entry in this sweepstakes indicates your awareness of the Official Rules. Winners who are residents of Canada must answer correctly a time-related arithmetical skill-testing question to qualify. First Prize winner will be notified by certified mail and must submit an Affidavit of Compliance within 10 days of notification. Returned Affidavits or prizes that are refused or undeliverable will result in alternative names being randomly drawn. Winners may be asked for use of their name and photo at no additional compensation.

5. For a First Prize winner list, send a stamped self-addressed envelope postmarked by September 30, 1985. In Canada, mail to Silhouette Diamond Contest Winner, Suite 309, 238 Davenport Road, Toronto, Ontario M5R 1J6. In the United States, mail to Silhouette Diamond Contest Winner, P.O. Box 182, Bowling Green Station, New York, NY 10274. This offer will appear in Silhouette publications and at participating retailers. Offer void in Quebec and subject to all Federal, Provincial, State and Municipal laws and regulations and wherever prohibited or restricted by law.

Enjoy romance and passion, larger-than-life...

Now, thrill to 4 Silhouette Intimate Moments novels (a $9.00 value)— ABSOLUTELY FREE!

If you want more passionate sensual romance, then Silhouette Intimate Moments novels are for you!

In every 256-page book, you'll find romance that's electrifying...involving... and intense. And now, these larger-than-life romances can come into your home every month!

4 FREE books as your introduction.

Act now and we'll send you four thrilling Silhouette Intimate Moments novels. They're our gift to introduce you to our convenient home subscription service. Every month, we'll send you four new Silhouette Intimate Moments books. Look them over for 15 days. If you keep them, pay just $9.00 for all four. Or return them at no charge.

We'll mail your books to you *as soon as they are published.* Plus, with every shipment, you'll receive the Silhouette Books Newsletter absolutely free. *And Silhouette Intimate Moments is delivered free.*

Mail the coupon today and start receiving Silhouette Intimate Moments. Romance novels for women...not girls.

Silhouette Intimate Moments

Silhouette Intimate Moments™
120 Brighton Road, P.O. Box 5084, Clifton, N.J. 07015-5084

☐ YES! Please send me FREE and without obligation, 4 exciting Silhouette Intimate Moments romance novels. Unless you hear from me after I receive my 4 FREE books, please send 4 new Silhouette Intimate Moments novels to preview each month. I understand that you will bill me $2.25 each for a total of $9.00—with no additional shipping, handling or other charges. **There is no minimum number of books to buy and I may cancel anytime I wish. The first 4 books are mine to keep, even if I never take a single additional book.**

☐ Mrs. ☐ Miss ☐ Ms. ☐ Mr.   BMS225

Name _____ (please print) _____

Address _____ Apt. # _____

City ( ) _____ State _____ Zip _____

Area Code _____ Telephone Number _____

Signature (if under 18, parent or guardian must sign) _____

This offer limited to one per customer. Terms and prices subject
to change. Your enrollment is subject to acceptance by Silhouette Books.

SILHOUETTE INSPIRATIONS is a trademark and service mark.

IM-OP-A

READERS' COMMENTS ON SILHOUETTE SPECIAL EDITIONS:

"I just finished reading the first six Silhouette Special Edition Books and I had to take the opportunity to write you and tell you how much I enjoyed them. I enjoyed all the authors in this series. Best wishes on your Silhouette Special Editions line and many thanks."

—B.H.*, Jackson, OH

"The Special Editions are really special and I enjoyed them very much! I am looking forward to next month's books."

—R.M.W.*, Melbourne, FL

"I've just finished reading four of your first six Special Editions and I enjoyed them very much. I like the more sensual detail and longer stories. I will look forward each month to your new Special Editions."

—L.S.*, Visalia, CA

"Silhouette Special Editions are — 1.) Superb! 2.) Great! 3.) Delicious! 4.) Fantastic! . . . Did I leave anything out? These are books that an adult woman can read . . . I love them!"

—H.C.*, Monterey Park, CA

*names available on request